The Unnamed Press
P.O. Box 411272
Los Angeles, CA 90041

Published in North America by The Unnamed Press.

1 3 5 7 9 10 8 6 4 2

Copyright © 2016 by Joe Halstead

ISBN: 978-1-944700-04-1

Library of Congress Control Number: 2016960490

This book is distributed by Publishers Group West

Cover design & typeset by Jaya Nicely

WEST VIRGINIA

Joe Halstead

a novel

The Unnamed Press
Los Angeles, CA

For Molly

ON A TERRACE IN GRAMERCY, Jamie Paddock took an arrowhead from his jacket pocket and ran his finger along the thin arc of the blade. He looked back at the dark apartment, at the unfamiliar people—mostly NYU students and they all looked the same: polyethnic twentysomethings barely old enough to drink, blank looks in their eyes, same toneless voices—and wondered if he was starting to look like them. Heading back inside, he returned the arrowhead to his pocket and then said hello to a few people he recognized while nodding to others he didn't but who seemed to recognize him. He ate some mushrooms and lost track of everything but a premonition that people were going to talk about him, and then he sat motionless in an armchair and everyone was familiar looking even though he didn't know them. The fashion design student whose parents owned the apartment asked him questions that he answered in a monotone and she responded by giving him a shot of Patrón. His eyes wandered over to the girls cuddling a vase of flowers, girls wearing Coach bags and sharing a bottle of red wine, half-empty baggies of weed everywhere, a place he didn't really belong. He was by far the poorest of the group, though it wasn't for principled reasons, and these were people who would've never spoken to him outside the apartment, but there, at the party, they loved him more than he thought possible.

You might be poor, but you don't stink, he repeated in his mind.

He walked into the living room, cautiously, to look for Jo, the sad girl he'd come with and whom he'd made happy by lip-synching Cher. Someone was crushing coke into powder and spreading it on a cocktail table, and when she offered him a bump he snorted it and the thought of familiarity or that familiarity was even a thing that existed had vanished. His only thought was the overpowering desire to have sex and that seemed to happen when he was thinking of death, which he'd been doing since his father stopped his truck on US Highway 19—five days ago—about twenty miles south of his home, on the New River Gorge Bridge, and climbed over the railing and stepped into the air.

Later, he was feeling sick, so he went upstairs, and when he caught his reflection in a mirror his face was a skull and there was dried blood crusted above his eye and the eyelid itself badly bruised. Before the party, he'd fallen into a cab door and smashed his head on the handle and forgotten by the time they were all packed into the cab. Rihanna, or maybe it was one of those Adele songs, was playing from an MP3 player and he was dizzy, and even though he knew, not from the intensity of it, but from the fact that everyone at the party seemed to agree, that he was having déjà vu, so that he could almost remember each screenshot of time as it passed, he couldn't do anything else but focus on the millisecond at hand.

He went to the bathroom and locked the door and then went to the sink and stared at himself in the mirror, wiping away the blood there on his eye. He turned off the lights and lay down on the bathmat, breathing carefully until he finally felt relaxed. There was a little light in the room but where it was coming from he couldn't tell, and then something flashed in the darkness again. It was an iPhone glowing, illuminating a girl's face. He turned on the light and looked at the girl in the tub. She was wearing a denim Levi's skirt and a wifebeater that showed her nipples, and her hair, which was burnt orange, looked like she'd just ridden in a convertible. She wasn't ugly; in fact she was fairly pretty, but she seemed like a squatter, which gave him a bad vibe. She looked at him and said he didn't belong there. He'd come with Jo, he wanted her to understand. The girl nodded and he noticed as she rested her calves on the tub that she was wearing a red thong. She was smiling, maybe wasted, maybe crazy. They talked and she told him she liked his hair and he said, "Well, thank you," and then she asked where he was from and he said, "I'm one of them West Virginia boys; you know, 'Country Roads,' coal mines, other side of regular Virginia?" She looked at him curiously and said, "Really?" and laughed. She asked him if he wanted her to clean his eye with her tongue and he thought, *WTF,* and then said, "Sure," and she did. She stroked his face and kissed him and then sat on the toilet, and she was playing with his hair and he slid her thong to her ankles and past her heels and flushed it down the toilet and saw her pubic hair, light and sparse. He was high and feeling good for a change, and they made out a bit before she decided she wanted to go to his place.

They left the party, and from upstairs in the hallway they heard the music calling to them and during a break on the track they heard fifty voices from the party next door scream, *"Release. The. Savage,"* and they looked at each other.

He lived on the fifth floor of a walk-up on Second Avenue between Seventh and St. Mark's, and he watched the girl's bare red ankles as she tromped up the stairs and then started kissing her before they walked out of the stairwell and into the living room. She'd already started taking her top off and had nothing on beneath it, and his hand glided across her lower abdomen and down around her hip bones to her cunt, two fingers easing into it. Kissing her, he kept tasting lip gloss, which took him back to high school, to a Dairy Queen on Route 19 where he thought he'd lost his virginity to a girl named Kate but wasn't sure anymore because Kate had run away from home and hadn't left a forwarding address. He leaned the girl against the wall and started fucking her really hard, looking into her face when he was coming.

It was later that she went into the living room while he slept and lit one of his clove cigarettes and, still holding the cigarette, stole his black leather jacket, which held his arrowhead, and then put it on, smiling. She went to the refrigerator and took out a jar of hummus and smeared it all over the wall and then stalked away, down the stairs, into the night.

JAMIE WOKE THE NEXT AFTERNOON, December twenty-something, dried blood all over his face, on top of damp sheets. The sun was low and coming through the window, hitting him in the face, and his arm, which was numb, reached for his iPhone on the nightstand, but the phone was dead, disconnected from the charger. He connected the phone and charged it, which took two minutes, and checked his text messages. He got out of bed, knocking a Burnett's bottle over onto some books from his last semester in college, and then walked into the living room looking for a lighter. He found the note written on the whiteboard and the hummus on the wall and then saw his jacket was gone and panicked but then had to stop and stare at the hummus some more because it didn't make sense; he couldn't understand what it was until he noticed the empty container on the floor. He tore the room apart looking for his arrowhead and then went to the sink and splashed water on his face. He couldn't even think about how the girl from last night came and fucked everything up because everything was already fucked. His father had been dead five days—no, six—and still hadn't been laid to rest because his family hadn't done it. That had always been their way. Time passes and people die and every day leaves you with less to say about it all. But Jamie could feel a clot of anger growing in his body. Gone for almost a week and still no funeral? His father deserved better. More than anything, or, to be honest, he felt sorry for his mother and sister: they were naive, and they obviously weren't taking anything seriously. They should've been planning the funeral.

But his sorrow didn't stop him from waiting six days to start looking for a flight. He wasn't a complete shit about going home, but there was something there that was holding him back, some reservation, some fear. It was almost Christmas, so he started thinking about Christmases as a kid and how he and his sister would sit at the bottom of the little twenty-dollar tree from Walmart and it was usually one of the good times. They'd grown up poor, same as everyone who lived in the food-stamp hollers, but they always had presents from Walmart or pencils or a video game stolen from Blockbuster. But those days had gone long before his father died, so he knew if he went home it'd be one of the sad times. He was, in truth, afraid of how bad things had gotten while being away. After a while, what he wished was that it'd all stop mattering. No matter how much he tried, though, it never did.

There was something else, when he'd spoken to his mother yesterday, for a second time since his dad had died. She'd added a new detail that she hadn't mentioned earlier, when she'd called with the news, something his sister hadn't mentioned when he'd talked to her a couple of days ago either. She'd said they couldn't bury his father because the cops hadn't found the body. And Jamie got frustrated with her. If it was true—and why would she make this up?—then how did they know his father was even actually dead? He thought about how he was getting older and how he kept losing things, things like his father, and how the more things he lost the fewer things he had, and he just wanted that damn arrowhead back more than any-thing. All he could think about was how he'd found it as a boy and how he'd promised his father he'd hold on to it forever, take care of it, never show it to anyone, and never, ever lose it.

He washed off in a long, hot shower with a washcloth and then went to the kitchen and swallowed a Xanax and looked out the window past the city, his eyes disappointed at the build-ings, and superimposed on it, his own reflection in the glass. He had an extraterrestrial look about him that only emphasized his estrangement from West Virginia, a look acquired during the six years he'd lived in New York City. He had gaps between his teeth, which gave his face a childlike look, and there were acne scars on his left cheek, which gave him a predatory look, or it might've been his cheekbones that somehow seemed too protuberant. He got dressed—jeans, black ankle boots, a gray sweater, a ceremonial trench—and then he left the apartment.

Walking north along Second Avenue to the fashion design stu-dent's apartment, texting, Facebooking, he wondered at the reasons he'd come to New York. As a boy and later, too, he thought he'd been born far from home. As if the whole time he'd been following a map, trying to get back, tracing footsteps and showing his face one last time everywhere he went. He'd come after high school on a scholarship to NYU. Vaguely he'd wanted to accomplish some journey, wanted to live in a room above a coffee shop with a rumpled mattress in one corner, a cheap Sony laptop in the other. Many of the people he met had come from faraway places like Brazil and France, but none had come from farther away than West Virginia, and after some time they'd been absorbed into Manhattan, while he held on to something, or something held on to him. He'd come to a kind of world fundamentally different from the one he'd always known and he realized such a world would require a different kind of person. So he changed. He started taking sleeping pills. Only Ambien, just here and there, but even so. He'd spent his nights at clubs or college parties, trying to return to a place from which he could begin again. More likely he'd begun to believe all the things his father had spent years telling him: *That's your home now. There's no coming back. This place will suck you deeper and faster than quicksand in one of them old Tarzan movies. You can't come back.*

Trust me, you can't.

He cut a diagonal somewhere above Twenty-First Street and the wind picked up and he put his hands into his coat pockets, and the traffic light changed from red to green and the red hand lit up and told people they couldn't walk, but he crossed the street anyway and then stopped outside the entrance to the fashion design student's building and rang the bell and looked into the eye of the camera and the door buzzed open and he entered.

Drinks sat on every surface and two girls, young and white and blond, wearing long cardigans and Nikes, sat on the couch staring at him as he passed, not saying anything. There was music coming from above and he walked upstairs and down the hallway into a large room that seemed to take up the entire second floor, and he stood in the doorway and watched as the fashion design student got dressed. She pretended not to care, which made him feel like a ghost.

"Thought you left last night," she said. "Fill me a bowl?"

When she said this, he turned away from her and she asked him what he was doing there and he asked if she knew the girl from the party. He took the weed off the nightstand and filled the bowl and gave it to her, and she started looking for a lighter and told him that the girl's name was Sara and that she did kind of know her but she didn't look at him.

8

"Well, Sara stole my fucking jacket, so..." he said.

"Wow," she said. "I guess I'm sorry." There was a pause. "Should I be?"

"Are you serious? My *leather* fucking *jacket*—"

"I just want to know one thing," she said. "Why the fuck did I set you up with Jo if you were just going to ditch her? You lied to me. *I am so fucking over the men of this country*—well, this world, really, but you know what I mean."

"I know. It was extra shitty of me. I'm sorry," he said.

He sat down on her bed and stared out the dusty window. Across the street was a construction site, a large pit ringed by machines that looked to him like giant monsters, which he found momentarily distressing. "I'm just gonna call the police," he said.

"Look, Sara's unstable, self-destructive, uncontrollable. She's run off again—not sure where this time. If she lives to see thirty, I'll be surprised."

"How do you know her?"

"She's my cousin."

"Then she has money to buy her own shit."

"Hey, chill out. We don't know if she stole the jacket. She was probably just cold," she said. "Why are you being such a pussy about this jacket thing?"

"Why am I a pussy for wanting my jacket back?"

"A leather jacket." She laughed. "You've been in fistfights and you have a black eye. People look at you and say, 'Look, there goes a guy with a black eye and a leather jacket.' We get it, you're a visionary, a badass."

"Actually, I fell into a cab door. But that's an interesting theory."

"What I can't seem to figure out is if you're the real deal or just full of shit." She paused. "Girls steal clothes all the time. Honestly, what is the big deal?"

"I had things in my pockets. I had this arrowhead—"

He stopped midsentence and didn't say anything else. Maybe forty-five seconds—an uncomfortably long pause—and listened to the traffic humming outside. "Look," he said, "tell Sara my dad died last week and I have to leave town and I need my jacket."

"Shit, I forgot about that. What happened?"

"They think he killed himself."

He stopped looking out the window when he saw her staring at him and he thought she was maybe looking at his eye but then he realized she was watching him. She licked her thumb and wiped something off his cheek.

"You can't even tell," she said.

That night Jamie had a strange dream in which he was skinning a white-tailed deer somewhere around Fulton and Nassau. He pinned the deer with his forearm and pressed his knees against the body and then angled a blade across its throat, near the jaw, and severed the windpipe and neck bones and sliced completely through the spine and then cut out the rectum and ripped off the ears. There was a woodpile nearby and for some reason he was throwing the guts onto it, and when he stood he saw his father dead in the woodpile. He dropped the knife and he was no longer himself and he watched the rest of it from beyond.

He woke up and there was a cry caught in his throat, and in some indefinable way the dream made him feel closer to home than ever. He couldn't get back to sleep so he opened his MacBook and compared prices of rental cars on Enterprise. He thought about his father. The police said there was no note. Only his truck, still running, on the side of the bridge.

In all things Jamie strove to be like his father. He'd never gone to school, lived in West Virginia his whole life. Claimed he'd only ever be happy in West Virginia and that no change of place could ever change who he was. All his friends could sit on their heels in their old age while he just kept on working, and he did so by preference. He'd been sensible and well meaning and always had a look of honesty about him. Tall, with good posture, a nice chin; a man who'd look you straight in the eye, friendly, but with a boyish air. There'd been something assured, Gregory Peck–ish about him. Jamie's best memory of him was the day he'd found the arrowhead. It was a Saturday and they were walking through the woods. He was five or six years old. The old logging road they often walked went through thickets, across a creek bed, and wound around a hill until it reached a pasture. Jamie fell on his butt and noticed the arrowhead lying under a laurel bush. Almost two inches long, the arrowhead's sides narrowed until they reached the tip, pencil thin, sharp. The right side was shaped with a precise curve.

"What's that?" his father said.

"I don't know," Jamie said.

His father took the arrowhead. "Let's see here," he said. With great formality he began inspecting the arrowhead. They stood on the path for a long moment without talking and Jamie was surprised to see that his father was smiling, apparently pleased with Jamie's discovery.

"What is it?" Jamie asked.

"It's an old Indian arrowhead," his father said. "They probably used it to kill a deer, then dropped it here. It's kinda cool, if you think about it."

"What is?"

"That somethin' an Indian did hundreds of years ago can touch us today. That it was lost by some Indian and wound up here to point us somewhere. Think about it."

Jamie took the arrowhead and pretended to inspect it. He climbed onto a small log that jutted out of the rocks. Standing up there, he was almost at eye level with his father. He'd spent his life thus far looking up at a mountain; it was the first time he'd considered how different that place might look from the mountaintop.

"Pretty proud of yourself, ain't ya, knothead?" his father said. "Let me see that again for a second, will ya? I promise to give it right back."

Jamie slowly handed the arrowhead to his father, who took it from him in the same manner in which he'd given it, and it even looked to him as if his father didn't want to take it, which made Jamie feel like he truly would get it back.

His father put the arrowhead in the palm of his hand and held it out. "You see how it's like the arrow on a compass?" he said. "It can point any way it wants to."

Jamie jumped from the log. "Wonder what it's pointin' to then."

His father lowered himself to one knee. "Maybe the search for whatever it's pointin' to is better than whatever it's pointin' to. Do you understand?"

Jamie nodded.

His father lightly swatted him on the bottom. "Let's go on home then."

It'd been a long time, nearly four years, since Jamie had managed to visit his father, and he barely called anymore, didn't even write—because that was, he thought, something his father would never understand, that there would be no use searching, no use having an arrowhead to guide him, if there wasn't something worth finding in the end.

At four in the morning, he left his apartment. The sun wasn't up, but he smelled the pizza from 2 Bros Pizza and felt a little better. He walked to a coffee shop where he had a coffee among a handful of New Yorkers with their historic faces. He paid and then lit a cigarette and set out walking aimlessly. It'd snowed earlier and he looked for places where he was the first to walk and kicked at the snow and then looked back at his fresh black tracks disappearing in the light powder. A guitar playing a folk tune drew him to a doorway with a homeless woman. She was unusually beautiful even with the abscesses on her arms and the blood on the tail of her shirt, and he walked away and they never said a word to each other. A few hours later, he sat in the public library and tried to write and then looked at flights to West Virginia on Kayak.com. He thought about his father jumping from the bridge. What would it feel like to hit the water below? Would it hurt, or would your heart stop on the way down? Something was running down his cheek. He wiped it away with the back of his hand.

THE NEXT MORNING, a Monday, at nine, Jamie went to work at his boss's apartment, a $6,000 rental, which was located on the Upper West Side and served as the set for Monster Media, the advertising company that created videos for other companies and that he wrote scripts for. The videos were very short, only three to five minutes long, all very simple. The company was quite a respectable one, or at least that's how it presented itself, and the project that he and the crew and his boss were hired to do concerned a manga convention that was to be held in Manhattan mid-July the following year, so he sat on the futon beneath the framed anime poster that hung on the wall and began flipping through pages of the script he'd written. His boss, a tan fortyish man with gray in his hair, sat at a table in the corner, talking about "specific changes" that'd occurred to the script after going over the e-mail log with the client. He assured Jamie that he'd be pleased with the edits even though Jamie didn't care about the project and he kept insisting that they could film a convincing "magna" (he kept saying *magna* instead of *manga*) convention without having to rent a convention center. And then the conversation took a more somber tone: if they didn't get the magna convention right, then Monster Media would go out of business. After that, Jamie looked at him and felt ashamed and needed a cigarette.

Within the time it took him to smoke, his coworkers and the two hired actors had changed into their costumes and hit their marks, and all of it—the giant katanas, the gloved fists, the Dragon Ball pompadours, the super short skirts with the faintest hint of crotch—seemed to suggest that it was thought out when it actually wasn't, and the anime projected onto the shōji chroma-key screens showed the eye of the "Great Mollusk," its pinhole pupil dilating, and a rodent with huge testicles dressed in a kimono, shamisen slung over his back, dancing and eating a bowl of ramen on the roof of a geodesic dome, and Jamie knew his world had become a fantasy because none of it really had anything to do with him.

At some point he realized the voice actor hired to do the narration hadn't shown up, and he didn't say anything and was kind of relieved since they'd have to postpone the shoot, but then his boss asked him if he'd ever done any voice work and if he'd want to do it. Jamie was good with his choice of words and body language, but his voice, that Appalachian twang, was the one thing he could never fully change. For years he tried desperately but couldn't quite strike the right natural tone, and he had a lying inflection that he himself could hear and he knew that when he was asked a question and had to give a straight answer his voice would betray him.

"I'm probably not the best choice," he said.

His boss laughed. "You don't have to do that much."

Jamie said, "OK," and flipped through the script to the voice-over and didn't know what he was doing there, and he was supposed to read the line *"The time has come to return to Dimension Z"* but was so nervous he tried to think of some way to get out of it. The director set up a microphone and some recording equipment and his boss sat him down in a chair and positioned him nearer the microphone and then the director, satisfied, said, "Action."

"The time has come to return to Dimension Z," Jamie said, and the *i* in *time* wasn't a long *i* but a shorter-sounding one, like an *ah* sound. It was the way he'd always said it.

The boss shifted his eyes from Jamie to the director and then back to Jamie.

"Let's try that one more time," he said.

The director reset the microphone and hit record.

Jamie told himself he could leave, that he could simply say to his boss that he wasn't a voice actor, but the words didn't—couldn't—come out and he sat there at the microphone, and the need to hear his own voice began to grow more intense and he didn't know why.

"The time has come to return to Dimension Z."

"You're saying 'time' a little funny," his boss said. "Let's try it again."

"Yeah, I'm just nervous..." Jamie's voice trailed off. He was about to say something, mouth opened. He could hear a helicopter flying overhead.

The director reset the microphone and hit record.

Jamie kept staring at the script until it began to blur, and when his vision became clearer he tried to say it again—"The time has come to r-return—goddamn it"—then closed the script.

The director just stood there and said something like "Wow."

His boss came over and asked, "Is everything OK, Jamie?"

Jamie tried to smile and said, "Yeah," and looked down and realized that he didn't have anything to say and tried to shake the thought from his head.

But it stayed there.

On a break and leaving his mother a voice mail on his iPhone, he noticed the director of social media, Laura, staring at him from the mirror as she reapplied the anime pencil lines on her cheeks and the garish blue lipstick on her lips. She was usually in conservative vintage dress that for some reason made him weak with desire, but that day she was wearing a Victorian military uniform with fur accents and a mystical amulet with a "moth" kanji.

"Don't you find the blasé sexuality of the rat groundbreaking?" he said.

"Yes," she said, and laughed, "a landmark."

"I wonder if everyone gets this much shit at the office."

She laughed again and walked over, and he was happy to see her laugh.

"They even wanted us to wear these fake double-D balloon tits," she said in her Australian accent, "like these weird gravity-defying tits. Can you believe that?"

"Now why would they do a thing like that?" he said.

She smirked but said nothing and he took a long look around the apartment. "We should kill them and make a *hentai* horror movie about it. A nihilistic Australian kills everyone at her job, buck naked, standing around with Goku and whatever. I'll write the screenplay. Make a million bucks."

She cracked up and he could see the roof of her mouth.

"So were you just nervous reading that thing earlier or...?"

"I don't know," he said, and looked at his iPhone. "I need to get out of here."

"What'd I miss?"

"Nothin' to say, really. I'm havin' trouble with this girl who stole my jacket and some stuff and I feel humiliated, and, just between you and me, my dad died last week, so..."

"Oh god. I'm so sorry."

"Don't be," he said, "things like this happen," and he was unprepared for a millisecond at her show of emotion, her attempt to make real eye contact, and he said, "I'm OK."

He put on his coat and told her he was leaving, and she told him she had tickets for the Joan Jett concert that night if he was feeling like he needed to do something, and he said he didn't want to get crammed in with a bunch of sweaty, horny old-people bodies where he might accidentally get fucked and then she smiled.

"I'll text you," he said.

"You better."

Later, he texted her "what's the plan" and she said the Joan Jett concert was at Barclay's and that she'd be waiting outside. He stole some change from his roommate's bedroom and then put on his coat and walked to the Eighth Street–NYU station and used the change to buy two rat dogs with everything and a Mountain Dew and then got on the Q. The train was full and he put in one earbud and listened to Fleet Foxes on his iPhone and he leaned against the pole and took a deep breath as the train came to a stop. He could make out his reflection, hair getting too long on top, sunglasses still on. He heard a child several seats behind him retching, then a splatter against the floor, and the odor hit him and he bit hard into his cheek to fight the nausea and that depressed him so completely that he just closed his eyes.

In Brooklyn, he got off the Q and walked along streets lined with dirty snow that looked like ash and he filled his lungs with clean, moist night air and his stomach settled. He met Laura and they went to the Joan Jett concert and got crammed in with a bunch of sweaty, horny old baby boomers, and Joan Jett was wearing a red leather jacket and looked like a bad clone of herself. Laura pulled a bottle of Jack Daniel's from her purse and offered it to him as she unscrewed the top, and he took a deep swig and said thank you and then handed the bottle back and she took a swig and he started feeling really good, and at some point Joan Jett got to "I Love Rock 'n' Roll" and Laura kept looking at him with those freakishly perfect brown eyes that were so wild and he couldn't help it and he was staring back, and after they finished the bottle he leaned over and kissed her and they went to her apartment.

THEY TOOK SOME OF HER Klonopin and he poured two glasses of wine. His iPhone notified him that a serial killer had strangled a runner in Central Park, so they talked about serial killers and looked some info up on their phones—Charles Manson, how he was from West Virginia (or had lived there); Ian Brady and his weird face; Dennis Nilsen, how he sort of looked like Mads Mikkelsen—and then she grabbed her iPad and they watched several episodes of *Forensic Files* on Netflix. She put her head on his chest and he thought it'd be nice to sleep with her, but that it would've fucked them both up and possibly their working relationship as well.

"I feel like my life's a failure," Laura said. "I feel incredibly scared about that."

"Why?" he said. "You should be president."

"It's just that I'm so scared sometimes and I think maybe—I mean maybe I'm next, maybe I'll just be running through the park and that guy, or some other guy, or an out-of-control taxi, will come up behind me, and what will my life have been for? I don't have a family, or children—I'm nearing thirty. It's easy to make a joke out of what happened to that runner because it didn't happen to us, but—"

"It's OK," he said. "I understand."

He hated when people got dramatic, so he started scrolling through her Instagram on his iPhone and saw pictures of empty rooms and animal heads.

"So," he said, "where're you from?"

She laughed. "Adelaide—south Australia. I really miss it. I've thought about going back. You're from Virginia, you said? Like Charlie Manson?"

"Yeah. Well, not exactly. *West* Virginia, same as Manson, so..."

"Scary. Do you get back much?"

"Couple times."

"Since?"

He shrugged this time. The last time he went home was for a long weekend to celebrate his twenty-first birthday. The scene came back to him: eating steaks at a sports bar with his father, the empty pitchers on the table, the particular way they had of addressing each other. Jamie said, "How're things down here," and his father said, "Place ain't changed since last time," and Jamie said, "And Mom?" And his father said, "Usual." He said, "What're you writin' now?" and Jamie told him, "Nothing really, not at the moment." And his father said, "You write some of the prettiest things," and Jamie couldn't really remember what else he'd said, but it was obvious he wanted to say a lot of things—the most important one being something about home—and his father sighed and said, "You're gettin' the feeling you want to move, right? You're realizing that you need to come home but now you're wonderin' if you can, right?"

Quicksand in one of them old Tarzan movies.

"You don't think you should go see how your family is?" Laura said.

"I was like completely taken aback by it, y'know? And I haven't been there in so long."

"Well, then, you just have to decide if it's worth going back to."

She didn't say anything for a long time and he heard the sounds of the endless traffic outside, and he realized there were too many things he didn't understand the meaning of anymore and he felt worlds away from all that shit. He smoked some of a cigarette.

"Say you could live in any time and be anything, what would you be?"

"What would you be?"

"Someone normal."

She asked him what was the worst thing he'd ever done.

And so he told the story of the dog.

5

GROWING UP, Jamie's best friend was Kenny Bennett. Kenny was a redneck and he talked about how he wanted to be one of the two toughest rednecks in school ("next to Adam Young"), even though he was kind of a pussy, even though they were *all* rednecks, and Jamie had a suspicion that Kenny wouldn't let the aspiration go until he did something drastic.

It came at the end of seventh grade. Jamie was in a sleeping bag in Kenny's backyard, drunk for the first time in his life, listening to Lynyrd Skynyrd, and he was feeling pretty sick and he tried to pretend that Kenny didn't say anything, but then Kenny said it again: *"Look at how big my dick is, everbody, quick, look."* He was in his sleeping bag and wearing a Mountain Dew T-shirt, Taco Bell sauce in the corners of his mouth, and his knee was pointed upward like a giant erection, and he pretended to masturbate, looking jumpy and excited, rubbing his knee boner, his eyes wide, a Dale Earnhardt hat stuck to the top of his skull.

"Y'all niggers have sapling dicks compared to me!" he cackled.

Tom Melvin, a "known faggot" among the boys because his hair was long and blond and his parents were college educated, was standing near the fire pit and he told Kenny to stop shouting "nigger" because it was the third time and a black person was going to hear him, and Kenny called Tom a dumb idiot because everyone knew West Virginia didn't have any niggers, and then he asked Tom if he wanted to suck his dick and that he'd say "nigger" all he wanted, and Tom said no he didn't want to suck Kenny's dick because he "wasn't a faggot," and then a guy named Ben Patrick, a skinny fucker who thought himself a badass because his parents operated a funeral home and because he'd seen the naked corpse of the cheerleading captain who was killed in a car accident, laughed and said, "We gonna do somethin', Kenny?"

"If Jamie'll stop bein' such a pussy," Kenny said.

Jamie's eyes rolled up. "Shut up, you fuckin' little retard."

Kenny sat on Jamie and started punching his head, and sometime after the fourth blow Jamie grabbed his arm and twisted it up behind his back but lost his balance, and they both fell to the ground and Kenny's dog, Rocky, a black bull terrier, came up to where the boys were, but the fire was behind him and Jamie had to squint to see what it was.

"Rocky," Kenny whispered.

Although Rocky was only five he looked older, and this was mostly due to the gunshot wound that'd mangled the left side of his head. He'd once been owned by the Bennetts' neighbor, Carl Holden, who shot the dog with a .22 pistol. The bullet was deflected by Rocky's skull and was lodged somewhere behind his ear. When Carl decided he couldn't finish him off, he turned the .22 on himself. Kenny's mother adopted the dog.

"Rocky," Kenny said. "Let's kill Rocky."

Ben Patrick laughed and said, "You wanna kill your dog?" and even Tom Melvin started laughing with him and then Kenny said, "Let's do it," and then everyone got quiet.

Kenny had this dumb scary grin on his chipmunk face and he reached past Jamie into his backpack and pulled out some baling twine and a roll of M-88 firecrackers he'd gotten in Tennessee, and then he said that one of them would hold Rocky down and someone else would throw the firecrackers in his mouth and tie his snout with the twine. That was the plan. And suddenly Rocky was barking because Kenny was chasing him around the backyard, and Jamie groaned and got out of the sleeping bag again with the realization that he needed to prove something that night: that he could be just as heartless, just as cruel, as any boy from West Virginia. Kenny pinned Rocky and Rocky was moving his body around, trying to escape, and Jamie took the firecrackers and Ben Patrick handed him a lighter, and he didn't want to see it when it happened so he turned his head and lit the firecrackers and threw them into Rocky's mouth, and Kenny, laughing, tied Rocky's mouth shut with the baling twine and then there was an explosion and Rocky was flipping around and his face looked like Daffy Duck after the exploding cigar and he was bleeding all over the grass. Ben Patrick said, "Oh shit," and looked satisfied in a sad sort of way, and Tom Melvin started crying, and Kenny, still laughing, picked up a piece of Rocky's skin from the grass and chased Tom around and then threw the tag of skin into Tom's blond hair and Tom ran around trying to shake it out, and Kenny laughed, and Jamie's hand was trembling and he tried to compose himself, and Ben Patrick looked over at him but he just looked away. He was about to leave when Kenny yelled something at him, and before Jamie knew it he was pinning Kenny by his sausage biceps and hitting him hard across the head and he wasn't laughing anymore—he was crying—and after a while Kenny didn't move and then Jamie sat there for a long time and watched Rocky limp off into the woods. Where he went Jamie didn't exactly know, though he didn't find it particularly hard to imagine.

The next night, Jamie and his father were sitting on the picnic table at the edge of the woods. The moon was huge, hanging low in the sky, pale, like the face of a sunken cadaver, and his father kept commenting on how big it was. Jamie knew that he'd heard about Rocky—his downward gaze whenever he came to the table told him so. They talked about it a bit, but Jamie couldn't concentrate on the conversation because he had this feeling that they were being watched by something lurking in the woods, so he looked up and saw only one constellation: Orion the Hunter. Jamie looked up at him. He never changed, never moved at all.

"Was it you that put the farcrackers in the dog's mouth?"

"All I did was hand Kenny the lighter," Jamie said. "He was the one who stuck the firecrackers in Rocky's mouth. Kenny came straight up to me and said, 'Hand me the lighter.'"

"Why'd you hand him the lighter?"

"I don't know. I guess I just couldn't stand to see him actin' that way."

"Are you lyin' to me?"

Jamie looked at him. All he said was "no" in a tone that made it clear he was lying. He wished for a moment he hadn't lied. Even years later, he wished he'd told the truth.

"Should I believe what you're tellin' me? I always have, but now—"

Suddenly their dog, Scout, ran the length of his chain and was standing near them and barking in the direction of the woods. He'd heard something. They stared at the dark woods for a beat and then Jamie furrowed his brow slightly and tilted his head and then lay back on the picnic table, his face covered with his arm, pretending to be bothered by his stomach.

"Think I'm goin' inside," he said.

"What's the matter?" his father said.

"I don't feel good."

"Are you sick?"

Jamie shrugged. Scout kept looking into the woods and then he started barking again. Jamie and his father turned around and looked back, and out near the end of the fence they saw a fawn chasing its mother along the fence, trying to nurse, as the mother ran afraid.

Jamie stopped talking to Kenny. He didn't want to hear about Kenny anymore and tuned out when someone mentioned his name. Kenny was arrested for statutory rape once but then got out because West Virginia is a small place and something like that'd hurt families. Jamie heard he'd gotten married and worked in a coal mine. But he never talked to him again.

After he told the story, Laura talked to him without looking at him, as if absorbed by something invisible in the corner. She talked about work and he was nodding, but the words weren't adding up to anything, like those books where people mark out all but a few words to create an enigmatic and entirely absurd poem.

"You sound a little nervous," he said, "or something."

"I sound nervous?" Her tone became harsh. "Maybe you'd like to tell me more about West Virginia and killing dogs, because you—I mean, I loved that."

"OK, I'm sorry. I shouldn't've told you that story, OK?"

"Well, yeah. I mean, I just don't understand why someone would want to do that. Especially these days. I mean, it's—you know—I just don't see the point."

"I know," he said, frowning as he checked a text from the fashion design student: "just talked to Sara And she said it was cool and I think she just wants to talk and work it out," and barely a second after it appeared he texted back "OK cool" and clicked off the screen.

Laura's eyes were half closed and she was buzzed.

"Neither one of us wants to admit that something's wrong with you," she said.

Jamie sighed and leaned his head back and looked at his iPhone.

"You're not a bad person," she said, "but anyone who tells a story like that without thinking—I don't know, you're just seriously messed up."

He laughed tiredly. "Seriously?"

"I think there might be something wrong with you."

He turned to look at her face. He felt ashamed, as if something actually *were* wrong with him and this wrongness were obvious to the world. He decided he was going to give the rest of the conversation sixty seconds. He nodded thoughtfully, as if mulling it over, and then said, "They told me I could be like all the other redneck boys if I put the firecrackers in Rocky's mouth." He poured half a glass of wine and sighed. "So I keep that story in the back of my mind for one reason"—lighting a cigarette—"to remind me of who I don't want to be."

AFTER LEAVING LAURA'S APARTMENT, he was sort of
drunk and knew he should've gone home, gone somewhere,
maybe back to the fashion design student's apartment, or
maybe to work on work stuff (he was supposed to write three
more scripts—one for a baby stroller ad, one for a lobster mac-
and-cheese segment for FoodNetwork.com, and one for how
to decorate a child's room for About.com), but he didn't want
to. He walked in the middle of the sidewalk, looking at the
New Yorkers as he made them zigzag through their indomi-
table purpose. They were young. Wearing black, thin. Walking around like they were supposed to be there. Like they
could go anywhere they wanted. At some point he turned and
walked down Fourteenth Street toward Union Square and he
went inside Trader Joe's and bought a deli sandwich with the
rest of his cash. He was cold and he ate the sandwich outside
and looked up to see stars but there weren't any. He walked
toward the 6 train station, half a block away, and suddenly
had a problem with the constricted space, with people standing too close to him, with tight landscapes, with too much
open space, too. It had to do with the sky-to-skyscraper ra-
tio, with space. He swiped his MetroCard at the turnstile and

got on the 6 train and it started moving through the tunnel. The train was full for that hour—there was only one empty seat—and he held on to the pole. He didn't know where he was going. The train made a couple of stops and then he got off at Forty-Second Street and went inside Grand Central and stared up at the decorated ceiling, at the constellations arching high overhead, at Orion, shield raised, sticking to it year after year, never changing, always knowing exactly where he's going, and the jazz music playing somewhere above as background noise had a meta effect on Jamie and he went back to his apartment.

It was two A.M. He couldn't get to sleep and then he took Valium and thought about his father and got about two hours of sleep before he woke up, seeing his father dead on the woodpile. He tried to go back to sleep and was able to forget the scene for a while and then the whole cycle of nightmares started again. Sometimes they were of the woodpile. The worst ones were of his father parking his truck and standing on the New River Gorge Bridge.

He was lying in bed and believed he was dreaming when he saw a shadow crossing the window in the kitchen. When he became aware he wasn't sleeping, he heard a noise and knew it wasn't his roommate because his roommate had gone to Texas for a week, so he moved to grab a braid of copper wire wrapped in pink rubber that he kept near the door and he walked down the hallway toward the living room, the braid clenched tightly in his fists.

"I'll fucking kill you," he said. He sliced wildly and slammed the intruder against the wall, causing her to shout, "Ow, fuck, ow," and then he realized it was Sara. His grip on the braid loosened and he backed away in the opposite direction of where she now stood.

"What the fuck, Sara? How the fuck did you get in?"

"Ow," she said, "you fucking hurt me. Jesus, what the fuck is that thing?"

He told her it was a braid of copper wire wrapped in pink rubber from his father that he kept near the door for times when crazy people broke in. Moonlight was streaming through the window and now he could see more clearly. She was wearing a black V-neck T-shirt and tight zebra-print pants and was smoking a clove cigarette that contrasted with the rouge on her lips.

"You are fucked up. You are fuckin' absurd—I'm callin' the cops."

"No, no, no, no, no. Look, look," she said.

She pointed and Jamie looked and saw his leather jacket draped neatly over the back of the futon. He didn't know what to say after that. Just paused and smiled.

"Thank you," he said. "I really appreciate you bringing this back."

"I had to see you again," she said. "I woke up this morning and ate a handful of cereal because I was high. It sounded like a good idea but that was the worst decision of my life—because I was high—and then I wanted the entire box because all I *really wanted* was *you*."

She took a step toward him and was looking at him through a filter of love and pity. He thought she looked like a Cranberries song that was too beautiful to be written. He was confused and felt wretched but was unable to pull away.

"Well, uh," he said, "I really enjoyed the other night and—"

"I fucking enjoy you. I love your corniness. I want to play in your fields of corn and germinate your corn. I forget what that term is. Thrashing, I think?"

He already had a medium hard-on. "Thrashing, yeah."

She came close and he was unable to resist her. Her hair was pulled back in a ponytail and he reached out to grab it—a gesture that widened her smile. He made the effort to stop kissing her, but it was, he thought, like when you see those burned-in patches on the backs of your eyelids after you've stared at a light for too long, and the longer you stare at the patches the more they seem to spell out something, as if there's a secret message hidden in them, some code being spelled out, and you want to learn it. She slid her hand under his waistband and grazed his cock and his skin shivered and she bit his lip. He took her tongue deep in his mouth and she had a metal piercing that clunked on the back of his teeth.

They went down to the floor and he tore her top off and kissed her neck and nipples and down her stomach, and she arched herself up until her back was a parentheses as he pulled off her pants and then spread her legs and he kissed her thighs and her breaths were coming in short clips and he never felt so good with anyone and then he licked her and she hit her head on the coffee table. She grabbed the coffee table with her right hand and his head with her left. She bucked against his mouth, pressing hard against him as she pulled him by his hair. When she was about to come, she ripped down his pants and he thrusted inside her and he came and she screamed loud enough he worried someone would hear.

Later that night, she slept with her head in his lap and he stared at the black TV screen longer than he should have. He touched the top of her head and felt two knots just above her forehead. His face was cold and wet and he felt the hypnotic rumble of the refrigerator's compressor vibrating the floor, and he looked at Sara and thought that a succubus might as well feed on someone else's blood and that he needed to remember that. Once she was good and asleep he got restless and started wondering where his arrowhead was, and then he went to his jacket and reached a hand into the pockets and brought out nothing but lint and fistfuls of old receipts. The arrowhead was gone. He became more and more anxious about the whole thing, even angry; he paced around by the window and then stared at his reflection in the dark glass and noticed his hair was turning white in places and his skin looked dehydrated. He thought about his family in the abstract—people without faces—and thought about how he didn't hate them, how he just found them frustrating, or so he told himself.

ON CHRISTMAS MORNING, Jamie got up and stared out the window and looked at the traffic going down Second Avenue. He stood there, nude, by the window and smoked a cigarette. He took a shower and kind of remembered the night before, and when he got out of the shower he checked his e-mail and then he dug around in his jacket pockets again, searching for the arrowhead, but they were empty. Even though he thought it might've reflected badly on him, he sent a group text that said "Merry Christmas!" to his mother and sister. He felt guilty afterward, like he was being insensitive, or like he'd gone too far, like he was just deceiving himself with all the banal stuff. It was all too close to an uncomfortable truth that he wasn't ready to face.

Sometime later, Sara woke, and he smiled at her hesitantly.

"Who are you and what fuckin' planet did you come from?"

"I'll tell you, but it's a secret," she said. "I was princess of the Kitsune Forest but decided to live as a mortal, so I came here on a giant fox I rode covered in fairy dust."

"That sounds very magical."

"It was."

Sara said she didn't want to act like a leech, but she "didn't think" she had any money and she needed tampons and tooth-paste, weed, and, oh, Cheerios.

"Let me ask you a question," he said. "There were things in my jacket pockets, things that mean a lot to me. Things I can't replace. Where are they?"

She scrutinized him. "Oh god. The arrowhead."

"So you do have it somewhere."

"You know what today is? I love this day."

He just stared at her blankly like he didn't hear a word.

"And I would love it if you spent today with me on Christmas Day. Spend Christmas with me and I'll take you to it."

"I need to go home." He'd been seized by something—what? Something he'd been trying to say for a long time. "And I'd like to have it back before I go."

"Great," she said. "Spend Christmas with me."

Again, he didn't say anything and she asked him about the arrowhead—was it his Horcrux or something? was there a piece of his soul trapped inside it?—and he shrugged it off. They shared a joint and watched a vaporwave music video on his MacBook: images of the World Trade Center in flames, a Windows 95 landscape with NYSE figures scrolling across it, crows flying against a scarlet sky, all through a bleak VHS filter. He'd lost count of how many times the red progress bar had reached the end and he'd started the video over again. Sara lift-ed her hand to type something into YouTube, saying she want-ed to listen to Grimes's new album, and he saw faint white scars crisscrossed with thinner red ones across her wrists. He took a hit and offered a tight smile and she noticed him staring.

"Oh, just—when I was a kid I was bored," she said.

"Really," he said. It wasn't a question.

They spent the day around Rockefeller Center and then, that night, for Christmas dinner, he chose Royal Bangladesh Indian Restaurant because he knew it was BYOB and he was in the mood for their saag gosht and two or three IPAs, but, just in case, he took a Mason jar filled with something that looked like red Hi-C from the refrigerator and they left. Walking down Second Avenue, he stopped at an ATM and got cash for Sara's forty-ounce Coors Light, which she bought at the bodega along with his IPAs, and then they walked down Fifth Street and the street was empty and the air was thick and loud, "thunder-snow," they were calling it, with pitchforks of lightning flash-ing over that Freedom Tower thing, and an old man emerged from behind a car parked across from the dry cleaners and he was homeless and begging, hunched over, his face burned, and Jamie gave him two dollars. They turned onto First Avenue, and when they got to Royal Bangladesh there were two Indian men outside, one from Royal and one from Panna II, its com-petitor, and predictably each was offering free things to get them to come to his respective restaurant, and Sara was about to toss a coin to decide when Jamie walked into Royal because its guy offered him free wine.

The waiter came and said the special was mixed biryani and that it was "really good," and he asked if they'd like some sparkling water and Jamie reminded him they were supposed to get free wine. They ordered saag gosht and lamb vindaloo, and the waiter left and they both put on their Wayfarer sun-glasses since the light inside Royal Bangladesh was disorient-ing and tended to make everything look the same reddish color. The waiter brought their wine a bit later and Jamie remembered that he had, at some point, touched two hornlike calcifications on the top of Sara's head.

"Why are there, um, knots on the top of your head?" he said.

"Well, if you must know," she said, then in a dull mono-tone: "I'm the first of a brilliant new species of human spawned by climate change. I'm supposed to breed with you humans to fast-track the advancement of our species until we start our new society."

"Oh my god, you're such a fuckin' weirdo, you know that?"

"Yeah, well, we're stronger than you and we'll subjugate you by whatever means necessary. Even sexually," she insisted, "which is the mating preference of our females. We're capable of unspeakable evil, much like a human sociopath."

He just looked at her with this *WTF?* expression.

"Hey, I'm a child of the nineties," and then, looking away as if not wanting him to hear her, "Look, I'm sorry. I fucked up. I'm not perfect, but I'm trying."

"I mean, it's—I mean, I just want my shit back."

"Your arrowhead."

"Yeah." He felt self-conscious. "My arrowhead."

"Yeah, so, what's up with that thing anyway? Oh god." She stopped, a look of horror on her face. "It was *his*. He gave it to you."

"Where is it?" he said instead of answering.

"I'm just trying to help you. It only makes it harder if you won't talk."

"I know," he said. "I know you're trying to help. And it's really nice. You're a nice person. But I just don't know what to say right now."

"What was his name?"

"What?"

"Your dad. What was his name?"

He wanted very badly to say it. Instead: "I need you to give it to me."

Eventually the waiter brought their food and then he said he'd forgotten to ask to see their IDs earlier, so he looked at Sara's and nodded and then they started eating.

"My cousin told me about what happened," Sara said.

He took this in. "She did, did she?"

"Yeah, and I wanted to tell you I felt weird hearing about your dad and stuff since I didn't know you and whatever. But I was like, 'He looks so sad'; I don't know if I've ever met someone sad-looking like you. Not much comes out of your mouth, but your face"—she paused—"it says a lot. Like there's this big hole there. Anyway, I'm really sorry."

"Well, I appreciate that, Sara."

They ate in silence for a minute. Jamie finished his saag gosht, took a swallow of beer, and told Sara that he'd like to just go home and get stoned. She started getting emotional and he asked her what was wrong, and though she couldn't seem to say what was bothering her, she told him that everything was absurd and therefore she felt like her personality made sense.

"People think I'm just weird and different, but I think I'm responding to how nothing makes sense," she said. "It seems like no one realizes what's happening. Like they all have this terminal illness they don't know about, or like there's a tsunami behind them and they haven't noticed it yet."

"Really—people try to wear all these hats but there's nothing under them."

"Yeah, I think we might need to get berets," she said, squinting at his head for a few seconds. "Or maybe you might prefer an admiral's cap."

He burst out laughing and she smiled her perfect smile and then he smiled right back without the slightest reservation, like a goofball.

She took a deep breath. "Is it weird that I want to know why?"

"Why what?"

"Why he did it."

"You mean my dad?"

"It's just that I really want to know right now. It's like killing me. I promise I'll give you your arrowhead back if you find out why."

He shrugged and wiped his hands on a napkin. "Well, I really don't... I'm really not too crazy about this right now. I really just want to forget about it. For now."

"It's OK, I'm sorry," she said. It was sincere, almost timid. "I know you're upset. I understand your pain. I've felt pain like this before."

"Well, you can talk about it. If you want. Your pain."

She smiled and took another deep breath, as if she were about to tread on some holy ground. "You know, my dad believes we have power animals that guide our spirit."

"You think so? What would you say mine is?"

"You're a panther if I've ever seen one."

She pouted her lips in this goofy way. He thought it was fascinating, the way she tried to make herself seem less attractive and in doing so made herself more attractive.

"So what does that make you?"

"Well," she said, "I've been told I'm a wolf, but tonight? Tonight, I'm pretending to be a panther."

The waiter brought out the mukhwas and Sara said she didn't want to put a spoon that had been in some stranger's mouth into hers, and he laughed and told her she didn't put the spoon in her mouth, and for the first time she laughed and he liked it and asked how her food was.

"I thought the vindaloo was really, really... you know," she paused, "good." She looked down at her iPhone and seemed to think there was a Christmas pharm party at some squat, 337 Broome, an old event space that a Wall Street Robin Hood had bought and given to UHAB, and asked if he wanted to go.

He murmured, "We can. I don't really care." His tone changed. "I said you could talk about your problems. Are you gonna tell me or like what's the deal?"

She smiled a sad smile. "I'm sure I'll tell you all about it someday."

Much later that night, in his apartment, she moved closer and whispered, "You're so lonely," with a sad expression that made her irresistible, and then she kissed him and whispered it again and he said, "Sara..." and she pretended not to hear him and then she went under the sheets and took him into her mouth and as her throat relaxed he groaned with relief as he shot into her throat. He turned out the light and held Sara and then tried to sleep, but the music playing next door, "Empire State of Mind" by Jay Z with Alicia Keys, reminded him of something and then the feeling disappeared and he started to wonder if he could go back, if he could simply get up and go home. He looked down at Sara and wondered what she'd do. He knew he couldn't go; he knew he shouldn't, but he *wanted* to go. But first he needed his arrowhead.

He went into the living room and noticed Sara's purse, which she'd left on the futon, and looked through it. There were a lot of cigarettes in it and tampons and the usual crumpled dollar bills. There were pictures of her family, her mother and father. He was picking up an invoice from a garage when he saw his arrowhead at the bottom of the purse, just within his reach. He grabbed it and felt, despite his anxiety, deeply calm and glad to be holding it again. He went back into the bedroom and got dressed, and he didn't know what he was doing and then he looked down at Sara, who was smiling dumbly in her sleep, and for a moment felt a slight dizziness. He walked outside and felt something in him *collapse*, and it was so cold that everything—the air, the music around him—felt frozen, and for some reason the people passing by looked like translucent goblins in the fluorescent lighting. Walking to Astor Place and unable to shake the feeling that he was afraid of the constricted space, he took out his iPhone and opened the Amtrak app and bought a ticket to the station in Prince, West Virginia, and then he hailed a cab and got inside and was gripping his iPhone so tightly he could barely feel his hand and a moment of doubt arose as the shadow of the city loomed against the window.

And then he told the driver, "Penn Station."

HEADING SOUTH THE NEXT MORNING, Jamie watched through the window of the Amtrak and saw the skyline of New York and its steel skyscrapers disappear—the city turning into country. Later, he noticed the piles of snow blanketing everything and there was a darkness to the world as the train turned west and left Washington, DC. He thought about how his life seemed like a terrifying series of smash cuts, and, after a twelve-dollar personal pizza and a cup of black coffee in the dining car, the tracks wavered slowly ahead past Charlottesville and the landscape closed off. The train continued through it in the general direction of West Virginia until the markings of civilization ended in acres of dark woods and hollers and freshly dug strip mines resembling, he thought, enormous graves large enough to bury a race of ten-thousand-pound people. In the dark, he couldn't make out the mountains, only black, asymmetrical varieties of shadowy apexes, and when he was the last person left in the car after thirteen hours, the train's lights lit up the next stop and he finally saw the rickety mid-twentieth-century lettering erected across its roof, identifying it as the Prince, West Virginia, station.

9

INSIDE PRINCE STATION, Jamie texted his sister, Carol, "can u come pick me up I'll pay u," and he looked at all the maps of West Virginia tacked on the wall and traced his finger along Milton, which was the town where one of West Virginia's greatest writers, Breece Pancake, was buried, and he thought about how he'd always wanted to take something to Breece's grave. He was struck by how fucking *quiet* it was and then he lay on his back on two of the plastic chairs lining the sides of the room and he stared at the ceiling and had no concept of time because his iPhone had died, but he assumed he'd been lying there for something like an hour before he got up and walked out to the parking lot to smoke. He lit a cigarette and there was the peculiar scent of the place: asphalt and gasoline, industry, and fossils. The smell of West Virginia was what a vampire must smell like, he thought. He looked up at the mountain across the two-lane road, to the point where it met the sky in a kind of wet brown corduroy. There were single-wide trailers and rusted farm equipment and old barns going up the side. A white dog stumbled down from the mountain. A fog hung above the earth, causing the dog to appear to levitate rather than walk, and the dog came down from the mountain and lapped at the orange water on the side of the road while ticks bulged from its flesh. About this time, headlights hit him and a red Chevy Cobalt pulled into the parking lot, and when he looked at the woman behind the wheel he barely recognized her as his sister, Carol. He got in the car and looked at her. Her hair had been cut recently—short on the top and shorter on the sides—and it made her ears look big and was the hair of someone who'd just woken at the end of a night filled with nightmares, and she was dressed in an American Eagle coat that probably cost $200.

"Hey," he said.

"Hey."

"Jesus, it's fuckin' cold down here."

"Ain't so bad this week. There was a blizzard. Radio was sayin' a dusting; weathermen lied again. Didn't have no power for eleven days. Governor declared a state of emergency. These power-line guys came from as far away as New York, actually."

"Wow," he said. "Sounds pretty bad."

"It was like a kind of future winter."

"Thanks for gettin' me." He glanced at her. "Haven't seen you in a long time."

"Yeah," she replied. "I thought you'd forget me by now."

He tried to smile. "Wha'd'ya mean, forget about you?"

After the conversation started and ended itself, they headed southwest on 41 toward Beckley and he sat, face to the window, head shaking a slow *no, no, no* at severed power lines, blackened store fronts, and the occasional abandoned car, and there were a few houses but each one had an old-style furnace with an ugly chimney belching smoke. Layers of coal soot had settled on the walls, the roads, and the trees, and the people's clothes and the coats of stray dogs were black from the smoke. Some people were burning garbage in the parking lots, the dogs were running wild, and the half-dressed children looked at the passing car with eyes expressive of their own bafflement and ignorance. The car turned down Route 19 and eventually came to Beckley, and the overcast sky reflected a putty gray and a winter rain pockmarked the highway and there were long, straight boulevards of Starbucks, CVSs, Walmarts, McDonald's, and Applebee's to either side of the road and all of this, he thought, could be practice for the end of the world.

Their mother lived about thirty miles away—Mount Lookout—but when they got to Fayetteville, Carol took a left at the intersection and went up 16 and he knew it was because she didn't want to drive over the New River Gorge Bridge. It was a long drive through the twisted roads, and in Ansted they fishtailed around a tight corner and the rear of the Cobalt scraped the branch of a small pine tree that was lying on the road. He looked over at Carol and her face was gaunt, thin in such a way that she looked like a balloon full of fish bones. It was a face that looked like a bad clone of his sister, an agonized face, not the sweet one he remembered, the one void of any telling struggle. He looked at her coat.

"You workin' at all?" he asked.

She looked at him quizzically. "Why?"

He shrugged. "I'm just interested."

"I'm lookin'."

"It's tough, huh?"

"To find the right thing. It's worse'n it ever was. You got Walmart'n McDonald's'n shit, but me, though"—she leaned to the window—"me, I won't be doin' nothin' like that."

And maybe she wouldn't. He knew his sister rarely left home. She was a sensitive kid, antisocial but funny if you ever got her alone. Anything else, though, and she'd just clam up. This all really started after she'd been diagnosed with epilepsy at age twelve. She had trouble talking and stuttered a lot.

On top of that, people just scared her—she'd blush, wouldn't be able to talk straight. It was on account of either the epilepsy medication or the video games she played or a combination thereof. He didn't understand it, didn't want to understand it, really. Growing up, he just had to help her adjust, help her get past it. She knew she was at home in West Virginia. She knew the world was indifferent to her. She knew that if the world shrugged its shoulders it'd be enough of an acknowledgment, and she managed to articulate a vulnerability that Jamie somehow stopped relating to once he left for New York City.

He looked out the window, past the road, to the dark mountains.

It was beautiful and distant, like a postcard of heaven.

His father had said something once: *A person could get to hate that view.*

"Any idea about the funeral service?" Jamie said.

"They ain't said nothin' about his funeral, nor about his body neither."

He didn't pull his eyes from her. "So you think he might be alive, too?"

She turned her face up. "Don't get all excited. He's out there layin' someplace."

"And you know this how?"

"I just know."

A half hour's drive past Ansted, they passed the bullet-dented road sign that read MOUNT LOOKOUT—¼ MILE, and he craned his neck to look as they followed the one-lane road to the holler where he'd grown up. No cars went by and houses spaced widely apart were lined up around a bend and they were somehow unfamiliar to him, and then they came to the old driveway, no lights or mailbox, only a wooden fence and gravel path barely wide enough for a car, and she pulled the car down into the holler. He saw the trees their father had planted along the driveway and she pulled up next to the single-wide trailer he'd once lived in. It was a cheap arrangement of siding and tin, one door in the middle of its broad side, one window over it. She put the car in park and turned the engine off. He got out of the car and a light wind kicked up, moaning through the branches of the trees. The yard was covered with tall grass and bushes, all of them strewn with scraps of paper, empty Mountain Dew cans, Swisher Sweets packages. Everywhere he turned, more trees and branches crisscrossed his view. It was quiet, no street sounds, and with a growing sense of disorientation he looked up at the sky and saw Orion.

"Welcome home," Carol said.

At the back porch he stopped for a moment before entering, almost turning back, and then he walked through the door and into the kitchen and he saw the sink was full of rotten produce and the counter and stove were a foot deep in torn cereal boxes and Chef Boyardee cans. He looked down to see he'd stepped in a melted stick of butter. The paint on the walls and ceiling was stained with soot from the chimney and was peeling off in huge patches of brownish yellow. A circle of torn plaster and wires dangled where a ceiling fan once hung. A giant flat-screen TV stood at attention on a stand in the corner of the living room, right in front of his father's old red recliner, and there was a muted Animal Planet show on about the dangers of leaving the pack. A feeling of vertigo washed over him and he walked around the room, instinctively searching his pocket for his iPhone.

"Hey, Carol," he said. "Do you have a charger I can use?"

She said, "Sure," and he followed her across the living room into her bedroom, which had a twin bed and a child's dresser. The bed's mattress was old and sagging, and the dresser was littered with empty lipstick tubes, med bottles, other paraphernalia. There was a TV with a hanger for an antenna near the bed. He stared at his sister as she unplugged the phone charger from the wall and handed it to him, and then he said thanks and followed her into the darkness of the house, and as he crossed into the living room he saw his mother.

"Hey, Jamie," she said, sad grin on her face.

Janice was heavier, doughlike, and her hair barely covered her scalp, and when she trundled over to give him a hug he smelled garlic and lotion and something else and the something else wasn't a good smell.

"Hey," he said.

He sat with Janice on the couch and talked for a while. He had been away a long time, and they were nervous to be together again, but her muscle twitches probably had nothing to do with that. Six years ago, there were noticeable signs of her multiple sclerosis, which had been alarming because she wasn't old, and it was as if she'd been fast-tracked to old age in a matter of months. At the start she'd had difficulty moving and been tired throughout the day. Now her legs shook with an odd palsy and her mind seemed blank like her brain might've been made smooth. After a while, she asked if he was hungry and he said, "Sure," and as she started into the kitchen she could barely walk. Her feet were turned outward into something approximating a mermaid fin and it made him sad to see her that way, so he walked to the kitchen and opened the cabinet and saw all the Reese's Peanut Butter Cups and Hershey's bars and Butterfingers and asked what she wanted and she said, "A candy bar and a glass of water, I guess," so he got her a Reese's and then he went to the sink and turned on the faucet and put his hand in the water and it dripped in orange drops from his fingers and filled in the creases of his palm.

"There's something wrong with the water."

"You know, your daddy said somethin' about that the other day—let me think."

"Dad?"

"It was about this old woman who had her family over for Christmas and she made hot cocoa and then everyone in her family got sick from the cocoa because it expired in 1997." She looked amazed and then opened her Reese's. "He saw it on TV."

"He was a good man," he said, because he had to say something. "Well, we'll have the funeral services for him even though they haven't found the body, won't we?"

"I imagine we will. Why wouldn't we?"

"I don't know. I just hope to hell that isn't the way it goes."

"I hope to hell it ain't, too, Jamie. We just don't have any plans for him is all." She inhaled hugely. "Not now."

"When, then?"

"When there comes a when, I'll tell you. You're good to want to help us out with it. You know, your daddy wanted to be cremated anyway. He did. He really did."

"But..."

She looked up, reminded of something: "Somethin' happened before he died."

"What?"

"He went to the closet and took out some canned beans, but they wouldn't cook because they were too old—they stayed hard and I told him he needed to throw expired food out, that it wasn't good to eat. He never put the new canned stuff in behind the old so we always got the old first. Nothin' seems to last anymore. It's like in the Bible, the Valley of Dry Bones." She put on glasses and opened a Bible that was on top of some bills and started reading: "'The hand of the Lord was upon me, and He brought me out by the Spirit of the Lord and set me down in the middle of the valley; and it was full of bones. He caused me to pass among them round about, and behold, there were very many on the surface of the valley; and lo, they were very dry.'" She continued: "My say is, the Lord can give purpose to a wasted place, but not this place. There's just you, lookin' for somethin' that's not here."

The way she'd said it was so convincing that he just nodded. He said he'd thought of moving back to West Virginia many times while he'd been gone. She said there was nothing left. He told her there was still good in West Virginia. He needed to believe it.

"I don't know why, but this place sprung a leak years ago, and you want to be that boy who stopped the dam with his finger. But here, there's too many holes, and you don't have enough fingers. You just have to leave it behind, Jamie, with the past." She pressed on: "Hey, did I tell you we were gonna go to Marge's for a little 'after Christmas' Christmas dinner tomorrow? I thought we'd go to Walmart and get some stuff in the morning." She stopped. "Maybe chicken 'n' dumplin's? I thought you might want to, but I wasn't sure. Besides, Will just started working at the police department and he'll be there."

"Well," he said, "he's always been my favorite cousin."

"OK, maybe get somethin' to eat first?"

"That sounds good, let's do it."

She looked at him for some reason and said, "You look so sad," and the silence lingered and then she repeated, "You look so sad."

"I'm sorry about dad," he said.

"Never could catch no breaks, could he?"

"There's few breaks left to catch, I guess."

He grabbed the remote control and turned the TV to TV Land because he knew she liked that channel the best. When he was growing up, almost always, after the news in the evening, they'd watch a rerun together. It'd been one of his favorite memories.

"I'm sorry, too," she said. "He was your father."

They watched an *Andy Griffith*. She knew the episode verbatim and he liked the old feeling of comfort, the routine of the evenings, a time for healing all the parts that'd been hurt during the day. He liked to let the good of the day linger right up until bedtime while the sadness of every day would have to wait until the next morning.

JAMIE WOKE UP the next morning panicked, not knowing where he was. The clock on the nightstand read 6:15. Exhausted, he groaned and pushed his face into the pillow and then sat up with the vacant realization that it was freezing in the house. He looked down and saw the hard-on sticking out of his boxers but did nothing about it. He got up and found an old denim shirt in the closet and put it on, grabbed his coat, and took what was left of his Xanax and then walked shivering out to the porch to get some wood but saw that the woodbox was empty, and he shook his head, annoyed, as he muttered, "Jesus fuckin' Christ." Going into the living room he stopped in front of his parents' room and leaned in with his ear but heard nothing. He continued into the kitchen, making no effort to keep the floor from creaking, because it was impossible to keep it from creaking, and made coffee and drank it from a Styrofoam cup, but instead of warming his stomach, the coffee soured it. He took an ax from next to the back door and went outside, and the air was cold and there was a sharp bark and dogs filled the woods with their cries.

He walked down to the woodpile, which was big and set back from the house a bit, and the wood was cold and half covered with a tarp and had patches of ice on it from where it'd been sitting out for weeks. He stared at the wood apprehensively, half expecting to see the face of his father under one of the logs. He started splitting the wood, plunging the ax into each frozen log, digging it out, plunging it in again, and then he got a splinter in his palm. It didn't take long for his hands to numb. They'd softened since he'd last chopped wood nearly six years before. He carried armloads of wood up to the porch and his hands throbbed and he listened to the eerie sounds of the Appalachian wild. When he finished, he fumbled in his pocket for a cigarette and sat down on the picnic table his father had made, and that was the moment he saw the wood carvings set on a notch in the oak tree behind him. It was a motley assembly: a woman, a Batman, a boy, a bear. In the center stood a cowboy with shotgun shells for legs. Finally, there was a goat with the word STEAMBOAT written childishly across its side in black ink. He remembered that his father had been teaching himself how to whittle, and for some reason it made him sad that people like his dad had to do such things to express themselves. But was he so different? He put Steamboat the Goat in his coat pocket and walked inside where it was so cold his breath steamed, and he put a large pile of wood over a couple of Duraflame logs in the fireplace and struck a match and lit a fire and then his iPhone buzzed. Sighing to himself, thinking, *Oh fuck,* he glanced at the screen and saw he had two texts from the night ("you went back didn't you" and then "you're not mad at me are you?") and one from earlier that morning that read "gonna chug all your coffee then smoke a cig since you left ☒," all from Sara. He didn't answer the texts, getting a needle from Janice's sewing kit instead and digging out the quarter-inch splinter from his palm.

Half an hour later, he heard the sound of something falling in his parents' bathroom. He froze, listening as the sound of

Carol's TV came faintly from her bedroom, and then he bounded out of the kitchen and down the hall and he went into his parents' bathroom and saw Janice unconscious on the floor. He squatted and lifted her up and shook her, and strands of hair were sticking to her face and he pushed those away and he felt his heart thumping against his mom where she leaned on him. She came to almost immediately and her body quivered, shaking like a freshly broken branch.

"I fell," she said, and reached up and felt her forehead. There was a cut there and blood dripped to the floor. "Jeez, I'm sorry."

Still squatting there, he held his mom and saw the worried look in her eyes and rubbed her back to try to do something that would make her feel better. Instead, all he could think to say was "You need to go to the doctor."

"I'm just tired," she said. "I was tryin' to shave my legs and— I'd've maybe picked a different outfit had I knowed I'd pass out like this. I'll be OK, don't worry."

"You sure you don't need to go to the doctor?"

She shook her head and then stared hard at him, focusing on something. "Is your eye OK? I didn't notice it before, but..."

"Oh yeah, it's fine. Just hit it on a cab door one night. One of those big SUV cabs, you know? Stupid. You sure you don't want to go to the doctor?"

"No, but you can help me shave my legs if you want."

He took this idea in and deliberated, and she looked at the floor before glancing up at him in an attempt to hide her embarrassment, which he mistook for frustration.

"You don't have to if you don't want to—"

"Well, no, but—what about Carol?"

"No, Carol doesn't like to do it."

He got a razor and a can of shaving cream and sprayed the foam into his palm and rolled up the legs of her sweatpants and covered her legs with the shaving cream and took the razor and ran it down the length of her calf, and the razor was so full of gunk he could hear the scrabbling sound it made against the stubble of her hair, and then he pressed the razor deeper and the blade stuck to a rough place and he saw the dark line of blood and gunk trickle down her calf and he shook his head to forget the image.

"Shit," he said. He grabbed a yellow floral dish towel and, with tenderness, applied the towel against the wound. "You're bleedin'."

"Me bein' me, I guess, that's all I can say. Thank you, Jamie," she said. Quivering sobs shuddered in her chest. "I'm goin' to cry."

"Aw, don't worry, I'm just wipin' away the blood. Musta got you pretty good."

The Paddocks lived between two Walmarts. One was no closer than the other, and his mom and sister always held a debate between themselves over where they should shop. Carol figured the one in Summersville had smaller crowds and lower prices than the one in Fayetteville, so they chose the Summersville Walmart. The place was filled with the same familiar locals, pudgy and mostly white, doughy, buffet-stuffed, soft, and they were wearing extra-large Walmart clothes. He walked among them, smiling at their familiar faces, and they had some kind of gray dust on their foreheads even though it wasn't Ash Wednesday. He passed by them and they looked him over with confused expressions and it touched something in him, defined in some way who he was and what he'd become since living in the city. Janice was in a hurry and she leaned on the shopping cart as she pushed it through Walmart while crossing items off her list, Carol and Jamie flanking her. Candy bars. Milk. Banquet Homestyle Bakes biscuit mix. She looked at him and he stared back, finding it impossible to imagine someone more fragile. She didn't appear scared and had an enormous amount of resilience for someone with MS. In the checkout lane, he hauled the cartful of items onto the conveyor belt and she began an airy conversation with the cashier about how the price of produce, especially tomatoes, had shot up since Obama took office, and they laughed and exchanged predictions on when this price gouging would end or when the world would.

He noticed the Walmart cashier looking at him like she recognized him and he smiled. Her clothes looked old and her face was covered in what looked like sores.

"Hey, how're you?" she said, looking down, smiling.

He squinted at her and she looked back at him and he was staring blankly at her and suddenly he recognized her. "Hey, how's it goin'? How've you been?"

"Oh, not bad. Workin' here"—her voice became strained—"takin' care of the kids. I'm surprised to see you in here. You live around here still? Thought I'd never see you again."

"No, I live in New York now."

She calmly scrutinized him. "That's what I heard. What's that like? You like it?"

"Oh, y'know, it's all kind of, um, something." He laughed and it shouldn't have embarrassed him but it did. "Rich people, you know what I'm sayin'?"

She laughed. "You know what I always think about when I think of you? Remember that time, after homecoming, those girls believed...what was it you told 'em—really had 'em goin'—that if you all ran naked through the football field? That thing. I forget, but oh my god."

Carol looked at him and said, "What?" like she was scandalized.

Janice rolled her eyes and gave him a look.

"Hell, I don't remember." He laughed. "That was so long ago."

The Walmart cashier looked back at the growing line behind them, so she hit the total key on the register and said the check was seventy dollars and then Janice took out her debit card and paid for the groceries, and when the cashier spoke again her voice became urgent.

"Well, it was good to see you, Jamie. We should do somethin'."

"Oh yeah, yeah, you too. Yeah, let's do it. Add me on Facebook."

"OK, I will," she said, smiling.

Her eyes were stuck on him, and he loaded up the groceries and then Janice held on to his arm as they walked out. In the parking lot, he stood wedged with the trunk of the Jeep at his shoulder and shifted the plastic bags, propping them up with his knee against the hatch while he tried to maneuver them inside. Smiling, he watched the interplay of snowflakes and light: the headlamps of cars, giant Walmart streetlights, the lit convenience stores.

They drove across the street and he thought it was strange there were so many potholes in a place where people cared so much about their cars. At Applebee's the three of them squeezed into a booth and held the menus in front of them. There was something on the menu for everybody and the total usually came in under forty dollars. That was what made Applebee's the perfect night out for a family on a coal miner's salary. The waitress came and he ordered a six-ounce Bourbon Street steak, and Janice ordered a hamburger and an appetizer of buffalo wings from the "2-for-$20" menu, and Carol finally settled on an Oriental chicken salad.

"I see her all the time, that girl," Janice said. "What's her name?"

"Which girl?" Jamie asked, looking around.

"That cashier whose eyes were stuck on ya."

"Wha'd'ya think, Mommy, you really think Jamie's gonna remember her name?" Carol added, "I don't think he remembers period."

He looked down at his iPhone and saw he had a Facebook friend request from Brooke Johnson and realized she was the cashier, and Janice told him she always asked how he was and then spoke proudly about how long she'd worked at Walmart, "close to ten years," and he was struck by the velocity of time and he thought all the moments of his life added up to little more than the "previously on" section of a TV show. The waitress returned with their order, and the steak he ordered was crusty on the outside and bloody and stringy on the inside and his side order of vegetables was wilted and smelled like a freezer. He considered telling them the cashier's name, now that he knew it, but Janice and Carol were already eating their food.

"You still like Applebee's, Jamie?" Janice asked after a while.

"Sure, where else would I get my low-quality consumer goods?"

Janice gave a slight shake of her head. "Your daddy'd never spank you," she said, "and I don't know why, but now you kids're a couple'a smarty-mouths for him not whoopin' you good when you needed it." She coughed, then held her hands over her mouth and a dark wetness dripped from her fingers, and then she got a paper towel and wiped it away.

"Kids? *What'd I do?*" Carol moaned. "I didn't do anything—"

"I wasn't saying anything about you all," he said. "I'm sorry, I was just jokin'."

"All I know is when I was a kid I wasn't raised up rich like you," Janice said.

Janice and Carol ate their food and Jamie stared at his plate for a long while, a little confused, before deciding to eat it. Chewing the steak, he watched the people eat and most of the men were coal miners and they wore reflective tape on their Liberty overalls like errant knights.

"Well, Carol, tell Jamie the good news," Janice said.

"I get disability now," Carol murmured somewhat proudly.

He paused, confused. "Wait," he said, "for what now?"

"She gets a lot of money for it," Janice said.

"Six hundred a month," Carol said. "I just told them I had seizures, so they started sendin' me a six-hundred-dollar check a month. I mean, cold, hard cash."

They didn't seem to realize it was obvious to Jamie that Carol was lying about something and that Janice knew she was. Her expression was so innocent that he couldn't say anything and he wanted them to know he was genuinely nonjudgmental, but he could feel there was something written on his face, a disgust behind his indifference. "You been havin' seizures again lately?"

"She gets a lot of money for it," Janice said.

He refrained from asking why they weren't taking it more seriously because it no longer mattered. He smiled weakly and tried to sound happy, but his voice was flat when he said, "Well, that's great, Carol," and then he swallowed hard. Everything around him was vaguely shuddering and he kept picturing a hole full of human skeletons like in the dry bones story. He pulled Steamboat the Goat from his pocket. "But enough about us, what about Dad? I found these carvings out back this morning. Thought we might have them in the funeral."

Janice shrugged, considering it. "I see no problem with that."

Jamie stared at the goat carving. "Did we ever have a goat? I don't remember a goat."

"Oh, your daddy had one at one point," Janice said. "Named him Steamboat. He was a little bit ornery and a little bit loyal. In other words, just right for a goat."

"Steamboat the Goat," Carol said.

"Whatever happened to it?" Jamie said.

Janice gave no answer but the dropping of her eyes to her plate of hot wings, and then Jamie repeated his question and she answered, "I ain't seen nor talked about that goat in years."

For the next several minutes, they sat quietly, eating their Applebee's. Jamie didn't know if that was all there was to Steamboat or not, but he didn't think so. As he took a swig of Coca-Cola there were tears in his eyes. "I just can't believe they haven't found Dad yet."

"I'd sue," Carol said.

"Sue, hell," Janice said, "I ain't tryin' to sue the police divers."

"Assuming he's actually dead," Jamie said.

"You have a good soul, Jamie. Much compassion. But make no mistake: your daddy's under a rock somewhere, bare-assed and dead. We may never find him."

"Course, you never do know," Carol said.

Jamie's ears felt hot and they were ringing. "You know what I was thinkin' we should do?" he said forcefully. "We should go down to the river and look for him ourselves—that way if he's down there, we could get his body and make good on his funeral."

"Jamie, you're not psychin' yourself up to go runnin' around that river in the middle of winter, now, are ya? What are you doin', hon?" Janice said.

"Just bein', I don't know—thorough? I figured it'd put everybody at ease if we could just get some closure. Plus, he could be alive."

"He's not."

"How do you know that?"

"Because your daddy wasn't a runner. He was good to us."

THAT EVENING, they went to his aunt Marge's house, which was just up the hill from his parents' single-wide. It was a two-story house built using coal-mine money in the mid-1990s and the outside walls were covered with mounted deer heads. Jamie hadn't been there in more than ten years and he felt disembodied standing on the porch, and then Janice knocked on the door and Marge answered and said, "Come on in," and foolishly stared at him a moment, her face melted, doughy, loosened by time. With his arms loaded with the bags of Homestyle Bakes stuff from Walmart, he used his heel to prop the front door open so it wouldn't close on Janice and Carol and they went inside and he put the bags on the counter and unloaded them and then walked around the house. Its kitchen opened to a dining area with a table and seven chairs from Big Lots or something, and on the walls were more mounted deer heads and sepia family photos in which everyone, including the kids, looked like ghosts or junkies. Meanwhile, Janice and Marge stewed the chicken on the bone in just the right amount of sop after they dropped in the chilled dough strips, and Carol drifted, like she always did in social situations.

He wandered the house looking for a quiet place and went down the landing into the den where they all used to play video games as kids. It was dark except for a ninety-inch TV that was playing the Outdoor Channel. He watched two bearded men in orange hunting jackets stalk into a deer path where a young fawn was running. There was something in its eyes, a struggle to understand, as it ran in circles, and it gave a start when it saw the men and then sprawled on all fours as if that very second, by miserable coincidence, it realized it was doomed. One of the hunters led the fawn and squeezed the trigger, and the shot thundered through the speakers.

"Hey, Jamie." His uncle Mike lounged on a recliner in the dark, formless beneath a quilt, eyes hollow, face gaunt. Even under the quilt Jamie could tell he was half his normal size, down around a hundred pounds, and his skin was gray, and as quickly as he felt like a nephew coming for a visit he remembered they were strangers. Mike had been a hard uncle to live with, awkward in his affection and loudmouthed. Everyone in the tri-county area who wasn't a relative or car salesman thought he was a son of a bitch. One of Jamie's clearest memories of him was when he'd hit Marge in the face with a frozen steak. She'd forgotten to turn on the oven. Now Mike was vulnerable and it made him nervous just standing there.

"You still live up in ol' New York?"

"Yeah, yeah, for now."

"Sand niggers walkin' down the street everywhere you go?"

An obvious pause followed, with just the sound of the TV. To break the noticeably uncomfortable silence, Jamie cleared his throat and said, "All kinds of people."

"You still in school? Wha'd'ya do up'ere?"

"Usual, writing. Working at an advertising agency thing." He paused. "Workin' on a novel. Doin' a reading in Brooklyn next week for this story I wrote."

"Brooklyn?" Mike took a breath that looked like it hurt. "God, it's freezin'," he shouted, tugging the quilt up. "Are you cold, too, or is it just me?"

"It's a little chilly."

"I tell you what," Mike said, "you try that new jalapeño chicken sandwich they got at Wendy's? It's hot, by god, you better have a glass of milk when you eat it."

"I'll have to try it sometime."

"It burns whoever takes a bite of it. Whoo-wee, by god it's hot, though, I tell you what." There was a long pause. "I'm sorry about your dad," he said.

Jamie stared at him, slightly freaked out. "Did he say anything to you... before?"

Mike sighed and shook his head. "Before I got sick, ol' coyotes kept gettin' up to Gene's place, how come his cows were dyin'. Your dad went out with me one day and we killed us one or two, skinned one. But he was bein' real quiet-like, so I asked him if he was sick. He said, 'Ugh.' 'Ugh,' he goes, just like that. Said he felt somethin' open, a space in his head, like his head was a house and he'd been livin' his entar life in the basement, and he realized somethin' and it opened up rooms in him, back rooms, bedrooms, living rooms, upstairs rooms."

"What does that even mean?"

Mike went on: "Your dad—you think he was everything. Perfect, you know. He was my brother, too. But he couldn't seem to keep hisself happy and that give him ideas. And one'a them ideas..." He trailed off. "Well, he was a sad guy and that's it to him—he ain't guilty'a nothin' else. He killed hisself stone cold."

"You think he was depressed—that what you're sayin'?"

"Aw, shit—don't put too much stock in that." He whispered, "But if anyone'd know, it'd be you. The face you're makin'? It's him to a tee, boy. It's your dad to a tee."

Jamie felt a chill run down the knuckles of his spine. "It's everybody on occasion."

Mike merely stared at the hunters on the Outdoor Channel. "They can do anything these days, all the musk and night vision and shit. When I build these handrails I'm fixin' to build, I'm gonna go out in the woods all day again. Gotta admar the guys who stay out all day just to get one buck. Really, that's the kind of guy you want to be."

They sat there and Jamie began to notice the way Mike was watching the Outdoor Channel, how he had a faint and barely noticeable but nonetheless unmistakable smile on his face, and it moved Jamie to tears, almost. There are times we all imagine ourselves as someone else, somewhere else, and this perfect world has no logic except, of course, that it's perfect, and then we forget the perfect world we live in isn't the real one, but by then it refuses to let us go.

Quicksand in one of them old Tarzan movies.

Their eyes met and Jamie couldn't handle the force. He stood up and Mike asked, "Where you goin'?" and he said, "I gotta go," and looked around the dark room and then something strange caught his eye. Under the quilt next to Mike were blind-eyed pups suckling their mother's teats, and the mother stared at him and her eyes burned with hate or something like it, and then he started to walk toward the kitchen and Mike called out, "Jamie!"

In the kitchen, there was the warm, oily smell of chicken and dumplings and he sat down to dinner with his mother, Carol, Aunt Marge, Aunt Zelma Rose, and his cousin Will (buzz cut, small wire-framed glasses, WVU T-shirt, ill-fitting boot-cut jeans), who kept talking about the police academy, and Jamie looked at him, not even trying to feign interest, pretending to be pensive for a while, drinking coffee and smoking Marlboros out of a pack someone had left on the table. Jamie sat at the corner of the table and Will sat at the other end reading out loud and animatedly from the *Nicholas Chronicle*, its headline something about fast-food workers protesting the minimum wage in New York City, and he occasionally looked up toward Jamie or Marge. "Well, everybody," he said, "I guess Obama's gettin' his way. I mean, fast-food workers gettin' paid fifteen dollars an hour? I mean, you work at fuckin' *McDonald's*." He laughed with a contempt so potent that Jamie could feel it. "This is gettin' fuckin' ridiculous—I don't even get that. I mean, you got these fuckin' managers on Medicaid thinkin' they're gonna make a career out of it."

Marge laughed good-naturedly. "Uh, McDonald's should be, uh—"

"A jumpin'-off point," Janice helped matter-of-factly.

"Uh, no—I mean, *yeah*—a jumpin'-off point, that's right," Marge said, and there was a kind of tired lag in her speech and her words came in awkward bursts. "Sorry, Jamie, I had a"—she paused—"a stroke a couple years ago and can't... talk right anymore."

"Oh, I didn't know that," Jamie said.

"Yeah, then Mike did, too. Bad stroke. 'Bout two months ago."

"Ah, yeah, I just talked to him for a bit in there."

"I asked God to knock him down, but I didn't mean 'knock him down.' I just meant..." She paused, shaking her head in amused disbelief. "Sis, what's the word?"

"Make him humble?" Zelma Rose said.

"Make him humble, yeah. That's what I meant. But..." She was staring at Jamie with a look of realization that troubled him and her good-natured smiling was replaced by sadness, and, hoping no one would notice, she smiled again, saying, "I guess he got what he deserved."

Carol wasn't eating and neither was Zelma Rose. While taking a large gulp from his Mountain Dew, Will held up the copy of the *Nicholas Chronicle* and chuckled to himself, squinting at each word in the headline "Missouri Police Finish Inquiry into Death of Black Man."

"Am I the only person who sees the fact that if somebody breaks the law that they should be"—he thought about it, then resumed—"punished? I mean, this is insane."

"The races of this country are turning against each other," Janice warned.

"It's funny that the *Nicholas Chronicle* thinks we even care. I mean, if they wouldn't run and it's not a felony, they wouldn't get their freakin' heads blown off with a Glock."

"What about history?" Jamie asked tiredly. "Why are more blacks killed by police?"

"Because *blacks* are killin' blacks," Janice said. "Whites aren't killing blacks. Well"—she paused—"I'm sure they are, but they're killin' themselves more."

"That," Will said, "is a media problem. Right, Jamie?"

"Sucks when anyone has to get killed," Jamie said.

"That's true," Janice said, "but blacks kill more blacks than whites."

"You put a nigger in the White House and look what you get."

Jamie didn't say anything. He just smiled widely at Will and continued to behave, but he felt a shapeless, confusing hatred toward his family. He looked over at Carol to see if she was pleased, but she acted as if she wasn't listening. He told himself he could leave, that he could simply say to his family that he wanted to leave. But, again, he couldn't, and he sat there and everyone stayed silent. Zelma Rose looked at Jamie, and he glanced at Carol and then back at Zelma Rose and then at Janice. Janice met his glance and then worriedly looked at Marge, and Jamie also looked at Marge and then at Will and then at Zelma Rose again, who looked at him once more before saying slowly, unsurely, "Jamie, I've been stalkin' you on Facebook and see you're doin' pretty good with your writin' and everything."

"He's doin' very good," Janice said. "Stories published everywhere."

"Yeah, yeah, doin' a reading in Brooklyn next week, actually."

"Carol, tell 'em your good news, too," Janice said.

On the porch, contemplating the sky, Jamie started feeling a sort of dull anxiety, so he searched his pockets for a Xanax, Klonopin, anything, but came up with nothing. He looked back through the window at his family and was reminded of all the times he'd spent in that big house. Before he'd visited his parents last, nearly four years ago, he would've never dreamed of leaving West Virginia forever. You left because you didn't want to be too ignorant or too poor or because you wanted to make an honest grab at dignity. You left because you wanted something, but you were always meant to come back. This was, he knew, how you lived with West Virginia. And he knew he had to accept this if he ever wanted to be happy. He turned away from the window and made a promise as he exhaled smoke: expect less, always.

He took out his iPhone and texted Sara, "I think I'm going crazy."

"Aw Panther why do you think that," read her reply.

"My family is saying they couldn't bury my dad because they couldn't find his body. I'm starting to think I'm the dead one and he's still out there somewhere," he typed.

She started typing something very long. He stared at the animated ellipsis in the darkness of the porch. It was sort of dramatic, but he could almost feel her sincerity.

Her speech bubble finally appeared. "Human cognitive dissonance," it read. "Like we believe we'll see our loved ones in the afterlife, because everything is simply just a comforting notion, but we as individuals believe we will never die. But I do think negative thinking about death is just not good. Death is just a different part of life. And don't dwell on it because the time will come to be there. But if you do, know it's OK. And that our energies and everyone you love will continue on forever in a beautiful magnetic field. Of Fireworks."

"You're too nice to me," he typed, and hit send.

"Aw thanks bebebe you're the best."

Will emerged from the house and offered him a cigar, and they smoked and drank three beers and Jamie lied and agreed with Will's stupid observations about politics and the Constitution of the United States, and he thought that Will was always so animated around other people but so businesslike and impersonal in front of him and he looked straight ahead, avoiding eye contact, pretending he didn't hear him, and then Will said he was sorry about Roy.

Jamie ventured: "Have you heard anything about it?"

Will paused and then leaned forward. "Well, there was somethin'." He took out a Samsung phone and then opened the photo gallery and scrolled down to an image of a form letter. "Don't tell anyone—integrity of procedure. I mean, you of all people know that, but they found this in his truck—well, just look."

Jamie took the phone and looked at the screen for a long while as if it were some ancient and highly regarded work of Greek art. The form letter was from Tamarack, the local art gallery, and read as follows:

Dear Roy,

We would like to sincerely thank you for granting us the opportunity to consider your work for the 2012 Best of West Virginia Open Juried Exhibition. We are sorry to say that your work was not selected for the show. With more than four hundred pieces to choose from, the decisions made were quite difficult, especially when limited space is a factor.

Although your work was not accepted for this year's exhibit, we encourage you to consider upcoming opportunities for artists and artisans at Tamarack: The Best of West Virginia. We wish you all the best in your endeavors.

Jen Brooks
Gallery Manager

Jamie inspected the screen with some effort before exhaling loudly and handing the phone back to Will. He was getting frustrated and things were sinking in. He was getting answers that didn't seem to mean anything. He wondered if his father had submitted the wood carvings. Just the thought of it made him feel sick.

"You took this picture at the scene?"

"My second or third night of training was when it happened," Will said. "Looks like he was tryin'a be a artist or somethin', is what would be my guess." He put his hands in his pockets and stood there, smiling indulgently.

Jamie felt himself growing angry at that smirk.

"What the fuck—is this funny to you?" He was shouting.

"Now you shut your face. I don't have to do this," he said. "But I am. Roy was my uncle. He always treated me pretty freakin' decent. So you oughta show a little appreciation."

Will's eyes turned red, crazy almost. Jamie stared into them and sensed that he'd been molded into a brute in police academy and might kill him, so he backed down.

"Look, I'm sorry. Text me that picture, will you?"

"It's evidence now. So forget it. It ain't somethin' you're supposed to know."

"You know, you are so right. It's totally fine."

Will leaned against the wall, looking out over the yard, and finished the shitty cigar and asked, "What time is it?"

"Almost ten thirty," Jamie said.

Will nodded in sympathy and mentioned that he was going to a party at eleven and invited Jamie and Carol along, and though Jamie suspected they'd have drugs at the party, he had misgivings about spending the evening with Will and for a minute he wanted to say no, but then he nodded and swallowed hard, thinking that he might need it.

THEY ALL GOT IN WILL'S TRUCK, a big white Ford with black runners, and he drove fast on the blacktop past the grade school to someone named Boojee's house. Will had a flask of whiskey he kept in the center console that they took turns nipping and no one said anything. The truck turned down a one-lane road and they drove through deep woods and between high ridges. Jamie leaned his head against the passenger window and the cold of the glass felt good against his bruised eye and then he looked across a valley and saw a strip mine, a sprawling complex of earth-moving vehicles ringed by fences and old floodlights, and the two hillsides were scavenged, looking like dark circles under the eyes.

Just beyond the strip mine, Will goosed the truck up a rut road and along a driveway, and he drove until they reached a ranch-style house that had been designed without any sort of creativity and Jamie saw baby dolls hanging from fishing wire in the pine trees and stray dogs grazing at a pile of trash. There were many other trucks in the driveway and Will parked near them, and they got out and stood beside the truck a moment before Will and Carol started toward the house and Jamie kept his distance, trying to recognize the silhouettes standing on the porch. Will said, "'Sup," and the subsequent call of *"Queer"* initiated laughter and small talk about women, other women, gas prices, and Obama. Carol said she wanted to look for cough syrup with codeine in it, so Jamie followed her inside and smelled the stale smell of Fritos and beer, vomit and purple drank. Cigarette and pot smoke and the salty stench of sweat and bodily fluids hung in the air like a fog. Everywhere he took a step the floor creaked like he'd fall through it and there were pools of Mountain Dew—or maybe, he thought, it was vomit—everywhere. Welfare-looking boys snorted lines of Oxy that were arranged on Lynyrd Skynyrd jewel cases and doughlike girls in American Eagle hoodies flipped empty red cups and everyone stared as he pushed through the crowd; the boys had no qualms about looking at him like they were stalking prey and the girls had none about looking at his crotch, as if they'd, out of necessity, evolved in isolation like the animals of Galapagos. He followed Carol into the bathroom, where she found Robitussin. He watched her drink it and then took a swig and started feeling old and sorry for himself. He said he'd be right back and then he went to the kitchen and found some Mountain Dew, which he drank with a shot of Burnett's, and he stared at the big Confederate flag that was hanging on the wall above the sink.

Later, he stood in the living room area and Soulja Boy was playing loudly from a stereo and all the girls were trying to dance with him, but it wasn't sexy or anything. He sat on the couch and for a moment it seemed as if he'd never known these people. A very young girl, fourteen or fifteen, sat next to him. She was petite and lean and wearing a dirty tank top and no bra, and she had dreads and asked him what he wanted to be when he "grew up" and he said, "A writer," and she looked confused and said, "Oh, you mean like books—I thought you meant like handwritin', like calligraphy or somethin'," and she laughed as if she were embarrassed and it made him sad and he wondered why he'd told her this, why he'd given her this detail.

"Is this what you really want to talk to me about?" he said.

She stared at him, her face placid, expressionless.

In the kitchen, he drank more Burnett's and watched a skinny man eating a Big Mac and drinking a biggie-size Mountain Dew try to show his abs to everyone. He was about ten years older than Jamie, but he could've easily passed for the same age or even younger, and he had the "Go back to your own country" Van Dyke facial hair and a ponytail, and he wore a camel-colored Carhartt jumpsuit and a T-shirt that said HUG ME, I'M FROM ARKANSAS. Will was standing with him, wearing a pair of Oakleys and giggling mischievously.

"Jamie, c'mere," Will shouted.

Jamie walked over and stood there staring blankly at him.

"Jamie, this is my good buddy Boojee," Will said. "Boo, this is my cousin Jamie."

"Hey, nice to meet you, buddy, you drunk yet?"

"Hey, gettin' there," Jamie said. "Good to meet you, too."

Boojee opened the cabinet above the stove and took out a big bag of Jolly Ranchers and then started unwrapping the individual candies. He dropped them into a punch bowl of Robitussin and Jamie thought it looked very beautiful when the Robitussin began to dissolve the Jolly Ranchers. "There's gonna be an orgy tonight. You ever been in one?"

"Oh, you don't know this guy," Will said. "Jamie lives up in New York."

"Oh yeah?" Boojee said. "Wha'd'ya do up'ere?"

He hated saying it but did anyway. "I'm a writer."

"Rock 'n' roll, my nigga. You grow up here?"

"Till I was eighteen."

79

"Well, why'd you ever wanna leave all this?" Boojee finished his Big Mac and then opened the cabinet and reached behind the boxes of Cream of Wheat, into the far corner, and retrieved a couple cases of .22 shells and said, "C'mon, let's target shoot."

The radio played Lynyrd Skynyrd, Brad Paisley, Lil Wayne, old John Mellencamp, and they smoked some weed and got completely fucked up drinking that sickly-sweet Robitussin punch and Boojee seemed cool and Jamie was warming up to him. The shooting range was situated off to the side of the house and Boojee and Will left the porch with .22s at their sides, fingers on triggers, and Jamie followed, carrying the shells. As he walked across the yard a wave of nausea-laced anxiety hit him. He'd learned to shoot as a boy, hunting squirrel and deer in the woods with his father, and had a deep fondness for guns because of that. But it'd been years since he'd touched one. He wanted to make a comment about how he hadn't shot a gun in so long—he needed someone to acknowledge it for him—but he didn't. They got to the shooting range (Budweiser cans, two-by-fours, milk jugs, propped up on a log a hundred yards away) and the whole party loved it. They stood in a semicircle and Will was alternating between being obnoxiously loud and strong and reserved, and Boojee was loading his .22 and talking about the "Appalachian Dream," and Jamie just nodded at everything he said.

"Now," Boojee said, raising the barrel of the .22, "first you graduate. Then you get some girl pregnant. Then you start workin' in the coal mines. You can make like eighty grand a year workin' in the coal mines. That's coal-mine money right there. When I was your age I was makin' good money in the coal mines. It was true then and it's done nothin' but get truer ever since." Taking careful aim, he squeezed one off and a Budweiser can fell. "It don't get no easier. Only coal miners and car salesmen make it here and you think you gonna get to go to Applebee's ever night bein' a car salesman? Car salesmen don't make the big bucks. Your baby mama'll give you a few kids and you can open a cable account in their name, the water bill in their name, get them on Medicaid, and, I mean, you're livin' like a fuckin' king because you're workin' in the coal mines of West-by-God and that's the flat damn truth right there. You're the king of the mountains."

It wasn't the information but Boojee's tone that surprised Jamie. A few of his nuances seemed questionable, plus it was like maybe he knew that that life left much to be desired and that maybe he didn't believe any of what he'd said.

"You're a faggot—you're so full of shit," Will said.

"I'll smack the far outta you, bitch," Boojee said. "Let me see that .22."

Will handed him the .22 and he passed it to Jamie, who took it and swallowed uncomfortably and then felt a trepidation in his chest, and he knew suddenly he couldn't hit the target, but he didn't know how to get out of trying without looking dumb. He flipped the safety off and steadied the stock against his shoulder and aimed and then pulled the trigger, and the snow exploded where he'd missed the milk jug and someone laughed.

Will looked at Boojee and shrugged and snickered.

"Why'n't'ya do her again, you'll get it," Boojee said.

His tolerance was supposed to be comforting and Jamie realized he thought he was giving him something and the benevolent gesture reminded him of his father. He curled his finger around the trigger again and aimed the .22 and squeezed the trigger three times in quick succession and missed all three times and then laughed and said, "It's been a while."

Will took a swig from his punch and belched. "You're a good man, Jamie. Everybody says you're a good man. God is lookin' out for you from above, motherfucker."

He laughed. "Thanks. I'm gonna run take a leak real fast."

He went out back to the deck overlooking the backyard and the wide expanse of field leading up to the woods. The trees looked gnarled and black, and he sipped the Robitussin punch and felt like a sort of passing ghost, born to a people educated beyond their intelligence, unwilling to influence their world, knowing just enough to understand how miserable their lives actually were, and for a long, painful moment the things around him depressed him. He tried to relax, feeling the cold wind on his skin, but his eyes were drawn in Hollywood fashion to something in the trees, a black something up in the boughs, watching him, and then he saw many hands and a mouth grinning.

He looked for Carol afterward, dizzy and a little sick, drunk, stoned. But, of course, he couldn't find her. She wasn't anywhere. The ceiling fans were spinning patterns in an enlarging circle that was suddenly appearing everywhere and the lights were casting halos around him. He whispered to himself, "You're sick, you need to lie down," and moved to the back of the house where he found a dark bedroom. The bed was unmade; prescription pills lay scattered on a table and, next to that, a gold hand mirror with a thin veneer of dust. He heard the door close behind him and saw Dread Girl standing there with this strange, glazed expression that was pretty fucking depressing because it was clear she wanted to fuck. She said, "Oh, you again," in a corny, seductive whisper. He smiled at her, and as she headed toward him her dirty tank top came off and he felt a rush of lust even though he smelled the rankness of her BO. She started kissing him and making noises and her hand was around his twitching erection and then he was shaking his head and muttering, "No, no," and she said, "What are you, like a faggot?" and he said, "No, no, you're like fourteen, you're too young," and that was the last thing he remembered.

Later, he woke from a brief, dreamless coma to a thumping sound followed by heavy panting and then he looked over and saw Dread Girl sleeping naked next to him. He stood and pulled on his coat and walked to the door, still hearing that sound.

He moved uncertainly down the hall, past rooms where someone had turned off the lights, and he realized the rapid thumping was the unmistakable sound of thighs slapping against an ass, and the lights at the far end of the hall kept flickering and then he went in the living room and all the lights were off except for a flickering lamp in the corner, and sitting on the floor, a porno glowing on a sixty-inch TV in front of him, legs sagely crossed, masturbating, was Will, who saw him and whose face projected something like an apology as he glanced at the couch, and then Jamie looked and saw there was this shape moving in the shadows, a figure, circling above another shape, whom he recognized as Carol, unconscious on the couch. The first shape moved down her, stroking her, squeezing her, its short pink dick, hard and ready, and he realized it was Boojee and the whole thing became like a GIF from a snuff film, repeating.

"What the fuck are you doing?" Jamie yelled.

Suddenly the living room seemed far away, muffled, and he was trying to shake Carol back to consciousness, but Will was clutching his shoulders, saying, "Please, man, please, man, I'm sorry," hyperventilating, crying inconsolably, and Jamie said, "You're one twisted fuck, you know that? You and the rest of these people? You're all twisted fucks," gagging and on the edge of panic, and then he picked Carol up and carried her out the door, into the night.

He went as far as the blacktop and then he couldn't carry her any farther. He sat her down against the guardrail and looked around and said, "Fuck," and then she started breathing harshly and he looked down at her. "I'll call an ambulance," he said.

She responded with a shaky groan and something he could barely hear. Her voice turned gentle, entirely without tone. "I knew stayin' here was the biggest mistake of my life," she said. "You can't see your own memories. It's always Friday night, but you never leave home. Home is everywhere." She laughed. "I never believed in ghost stories," she said, "and I never wanted to, but you can't change what happens to you, and once it does..." She laughed to herself.

But he didn't hear a word. Her voice was the voice of a ghost.

Someone from the party pulled up and gave them a ride.

God is lookin' out for you from above, motherfucker.

When they got back home, he carried her into her bedroom and eased her into bed, and then he stood there for a second and her eyes opened and they stared at each other uncertainly. He felt sick so he ran to the bathroom, keeping his head down, and lifted the toilet seat and vomited into the bowl, and then he was pulling his clothes off, crying, and he jumped in the shower and pulled his hair.

13

THE TV WAS GOING full blast when Jamie woke up. It was Friday morning and Janice was in the living room watching a sermon on the big screen. Jamie sat in his dad's old La-Z-Boy, his eyes red, and zoned out while the preacher talked about how Isaiah saw God and said, "Woe is me, for I am lost, because a man of unclean lips am I, and in the midst of people of unclean lips do I dwell," and how Isaiah's purpose was not only to criticize his people to keep them on the right path but also to give them courage at a time when they were being threatened by a new empire. Jamie thought he should listen closely until the preacher started talking for more than forty-five minutes on how the races of the world should be kept separate and that blacks, Muslims, and Hispanics were "naturally savage people" who were "leading us toward an America without capitalism." Jamie didn't say anything to Janice about what happened to Carol. He knew he should've done more and he knew that his choice would be terrible enough that other terrible choices he'd make would be judged against it. But West Virginia was a small place and that was the kind of thing that hurt families, so he stayed quiet.

"You doin' all right this morning?" Janice asked.

"I'm all right," he said. "You?"

She smiled at the TV. "Not too bad. And I ain't kiddin'."

Though his aching head made him want to go back to bed, he thought about asking his mother if she knew anything else about Steamboat the Goat. Why would his father care so much about a goddamn goat? Was he crazy for even thinking about it?

He was in contemplation of that and other questions, like how his life had turned into a wacky joke since he'd come back to West Virginia, when some long-festering desire took hold of him and he needed, almost primally, to take a walk in the woods. So he left the house and walked into the woods with his father's .22 at his side until he reached the valley where the creek ran, which was the section of woods where he'd found the arrowhead as a boy. Here, he went to pieces, saw things. Visions. Faint ghosts from key events in his life.

Everything reminded him of the old days: the D-shaped cliff his father had called the Indian Rock; the cave where he and Bryan had found three sticks of dynamite; old Gene's field with its dirt roads and foundations that divided the parcels of land into massive squares. He crossed a barbed wire fence and passed the coyote that Uncle Mike had skinned. Reaching the top of the ridge, he saw the creek bed below and, twenty yards beyond that, the acid mine drainage that collected in a spring that flowed from runoff. He went into the creek and put his hand in the drainage as if it were something dangerous, or precious even. The substance was practically sludge, dripping in orange drops from each finger and sliding down to his wrist. He washed his hands in a clean part of the creek. *Appalachians fuckin' the shit out of their own land,* he thought. *Welcome to the beautiful Kanawha clear-cut.*

How times change, the things you know may not be the things you think they are at all. Time is a precious thing and it passes quickly and you never know it until the last second, which is the one second you cannot avoid. And there's no avoiding change either. One day you're a weird hillbilly guy who thinks Applebee's is a nice restaurant and who can't pronounce the names of famous writers and you're thinking you might someday want to write books yourself but you're too much of a chickenshit to leave West Virginia to do it. The next you're living in New York City and going to New York University and you've gotten far away enough to where you about can't call West Virginia home anymore.

Jamie, once insulated and unaffected, felt it all. Things had changed, mutated, and he thought his neck might snap. He had no idea what he was doing there and he kept thinking he probably looked like an idiot carrying the .22 in his long coat. He rounded a bend and off to one side was a fence that ran along the road and was posted with yellow NO TRESPASSING signs and underneath the end that was stapled to an oak was a salt lick. He knelt down and touched the salt and felt sort of sorry for the deer, because they were dumb animals who were always going back to the salt even if they understood that what they were doing was slowly killing them, and then he spotted a flash of white dashing down the hill toward the creek. It was a buck and his heart was suddenly pounding. He leaped after it and it bounded through the woods and he chased, the white and purple and blue of the sky flashing behind trees and under hanging branches. He chased it through brambles, scratching and cutting his skin and leaving thorns in his coat and jeans. The buck leaped over the creek and he teetered on the edge and then raised the .22, and the buck was in sight and he pulled the trigger and the shot thundered. Some vague ripple surged forward from a past he didn't want to remember. He'd missed.

It began to snow, so he went back home and walked into the living room and leaned his father's .22 in the corner, and then he went into his parents' bedroom to get the gun-cleaning kit his father had always kept in the dresser. He opened the dresser and got the kit, and then he saw a box with a bunch of papers and photos. It felt like a violation, but he figured his dad was dead and someone would be going through the box anyway. Inside the box was a photo of himself as a kid sitting at the top of a slide. He remembered when the picture was taken—it was the afternoon of his first day of kindergarten. There was a picture of his father with Janice at what looked like his grandparents' house one summer. His father was standing next to her, holding baby Carol on his hip, and he had a mullet and looked so young and they looked happy. Deeper down in the box there were outdated bills, Jamie's first published short story, old fishing licenses.

He sat on the edge of the bed, then took out his iPhone and called Tamarack. Then he borrowed Janice's Jeep and drove the thirty-five minutes to Beckley and along the way he saw blown-out tires and buzzards devouring roadkill in the ditches.

TAMARACK WAS AN Appalachian tourist destination where visitors and locals could indulge in goods thought to be found in West Virginia: art, hundred-dollar wine (indicative of no West Virginian), coal figurines, and luxurious handmade quilts, which actually were handmade. Jamie walked to the fine arts gallery and, stopping at the door of the gallery director, asked the assistant if Jen had arrived and the assistant told him Jen wouldn't be in until one o'clock, and then he wandered around, lingering at coal-themed works of art, and he thought about what West Virginia would be if the people would just withdraw their investment in coal. He went to the lobby and flipped through the self-published books in the book section, and at around 12:30 he sat in the food court and ordered a Greenbrier coffee and a pastry, which he didn't eat, unsure of why he even ordered it. After thirty minutes, the assistant came and told him it wouldn't be until about 1:30 that Jen would actually arrive, and she led him back to the gallery office where he could wait and then she left and he noticed there was a photograph on the wall of a statue raising its arms above its head like, he thought, an atomic bomb had just gone off in the sky. He stared at it a long time and something caught in him and he shivered.

"That's a wonderful photograph you're looking at."

When he turned around a woman was in the doorway. She was holding a Starbucks cup and was young, twentysomething, neatly appareled and nicely shaped with abundant auburn hair and a quite pretty face.

"Oh yeah, hi, hope I'm not bothering you."

"Not at all," she said. "I'm sorry I'm late. Jamie, right? I'm Jen."

Jen held out her hand sheepishly and he abruptly shook it and mumbled his thanks that she'd met with him, and then she sat down in the chair across the desk from him.

"You were saying about the photograph?"

"Yeah," she said casually, gesturing at it, "it's actually by this great photographer from West Virginia who's very quickly becoming our biggest seller. Anyway, the statue is a replica of a piece by a sculptor named Georg Kolbe that's in the Barcelona Pavilion, which was designed by the architect Mies van der Rohe." Her face creased with a tight smile. "Sorry if this is boring you..."

He shook his head and said, "No, go on," and she continued:

"Well, in the middle of this building was the statue. The fact that van der Rohe took the statue out of the main round and put it in a place that only allowed one point of view is an example of what we often do, on a larger scale, to groups of people. A statue by definition is the experience of a person that is converted into a frozen moment. The act of limiting your perspective to a flat image."

"That's really a beautiful statement," he said.

She said it "really was" and then asked if he was there for the skiing, and he looked at her with a confused expression. She smiled wryly—it was actually a sympathetic expression—and said she just assumed he was on a ski vacation and he said, "No, no, I live in New York, but I grew up here," and she said,

"Oh, well, welcome home then," and there was a pause.

"So, how can I help you today?"

"Well," he said, trying to hide his reluctance, "there is something...I mean, something happened, um...y'know, now that I'm here I feel pretty stupid, but... I need... I was going to see if you'd—I'm anxious to hear your thoughts on something that happened."

He explained his father's rejection letter and asked if she remembered his work, and she said that it'd been "cute, and maybe not bad," and then a conversation started about how the financial situation of Tamarack was escalating: departments were going to start falling like dominoes and even her job seemed in danger. He was nodding in agreement and listening and she was making helpful comments.

"My job," she said, "is to portray the effect West Virginia has on us, through our art, but also to meet tourist expectations about the shape our lives are assumed to take. Your father's pieces didn't really speak to that idea. I can't turn a profit without sales. The tourists are ignorant, to be sure, but they make up in funds what the locals lack in sophistication."

"That sounds like a bunch of bullshit."

"I—I understand that, uh, Mr. Paddock. I have sat in that exact seat so I think I have a sense of, uh... If you came down here to advocate for your father's art, I have to tell you: we're not going to change our minds on the carvings."

He shook his head and pulled Steamboat the Goat from his pocket. "These carvings, I know they aren't good. It's not about the carvings. He killed himself about two weeks ago. I just figured—we weren't... uh, perfect. We weren't in touch recently. But he came through for me, growing up. And I just figured I owe it to him to find out what happened."

She swallowed hard and looked to go cold. "I'm very sorry for your loss."

"I thought he might've told you something, mentioned something," he said, "before he died... If he'd been secretive about something, or, y'know, whatever?" He phrased it as a question so she'd have to validate something for him.

"There's his artist's statement... could be something there?"

"All right, let me see it... um, could I see it?"

She looked tired and her customer service facade changed; she was now sad. She sighed and seemed regretful and then she clicked a few buttons on her computer, her bloodshot eyes scanning the screen, and her printer made a noise and printed a sheet of paper, which she handed to him. It read as follows:

To Whom It May Concern,

I'd like to see if you'd consider my wood carving "Steamboat" for the 2012 Best of West Virginia Open Juried Exhibition. Sure would like to see it in the show, a friend of mine said you was looking for wood carvings, but if you'd rather not that's OK I look elsewhere. I hoped whatever my kids decided to do they'd live a Good Full life and I hoped whatever there dreams may be they'd come true. This wood carving is for all the things I did for them. And always remember the bad things you do. Like how I am shame about Steamboat and Cortis Pittenger. He was right about what he said about me all those years ago. "A change of place can't change who you are." That's what he said to me. The problem with trying to change yourself is you can't. People can't change there past. I don't know who the first guy to say they can but it couldn't have been Cortis. He never would've said something so stupid. I might be a "RED neck" but that's OK. I guess people have to judge other people somehow. Please consider my wood carving anyhow. Well I've talked too long.

Your's-Truly,
Roy Paddock

He read the letter again. Every day, for as long as he could remember, he'd felt a latent sadness, except *sadness* wasn't the right word. It was like there should've been a bigger word than *sadness* in the English language, but there wasn't a word in any language that could ever explain it. No matter what he did, it felt like there wasn't a person on Earth who could understand him. He now thought maybe his father could've understood him. His dear old dad who could barely put a sentence together, could he have felt the same thing?

"Thanks for your help, I really appreciate it," he muttered.

Jen produced a business card with various phone numbers on it and then she wrote something in the margins and handed it to him. "If you need anything, call me."

He took the card and saw she'd written her cell number, and he couldn't get over the fact that she still lived in West Virginia because she seemed more competent than it deserved. She didn't even have an accent. Maybe he was wrong about everything. He walked outside and smoked a cigarette and then he tried to light another but his hands were shaking too bad.

He left Tamarack and drove to Mount Lookout, and the whole way back he was screaming and crying and punching the roof of the Jeep like some real-life version of a stupid Oscar scene. Again he thought of his father in the woodpile, calling for him, but he wasn't able to get to the voice. It wasn't a question of where the voice was coming from. It wasn't coming from heaven or hell or someplace in between. It had just become part of death's chorus, and death is like having concrete seal you inside the Hoover Dam. He wasn't able to get to the voice but he could hear it calling. That's death and that's the worst part about the whole thing.

But what bothered him more, the thing that made him angry, was the name Cortis Pittenger. Cortis was a crippled-up Vietnam vet who'd lived up the road from his parents in Mount

Lookout and had always given his father hell. For example, Cortis once accused his father, then in his teens, of hitting him with a snowball, and they went to court and everything and his father had been found not guilty of whatever the charge was because there was nothing to substantiate any of it. Another time, when Jamie was nine, they'd gone fishing at Cortis's pond with the intention of catching bass for dinner when Cortis had his father arrested for trespassing. Jamie'd never thought about it before, but it was pretty pathetic if that was how the old man lived his life. He thought Cortis must've been one of those guys who took more pride in whom he hurt than in who he was. He wondered what Cortis looked like now, trying to remember when he'd seen him last, and what he had on his father.

When he got to Mount Lookout, he parked the Jeep in its allotted space and got out and walked across the yard to the back porch and then opened the sliding glass door and walked in. The living room was dark except for the weird anime that was glowing from the TV, and Janice and Carol sat on the couch and stared as though hypnotized, their blank black eyes reflecting the flashes, and then they both glanced up at him with identical, curiously calm faces.

"You've already been here," Janice said.

He looked at her with a confused expression.

"You've already been here," she said again.

"I don't know what you're saying."

He thought he could feel something in the darkness, a change in something, and the anime girl was saying, *"He hides who he really is and pretends to be someone else. So in time he becomes that person, so he transcends the mask, see? Well, don't you get it? That's how he finds happiness,"* and he took his father's .22 from the corner and started out again.

"I'll be back in a little bit," he said.

15

THE WOODS WAS COLD and stopped with a pillowy silence.

He passed by the shooting range at the road's end and then left the path and walked from there across the valley where the creek ran to Gene's field. He crossed the field and jumped the gate on the other side and then started down the hill and the grade steepened, the path gone, and the underbrush and branches closed in like hands that buried him with big loads of snow. The woods gave out to the D-shaped Indian Rock on the right, and he moved around a broken pine and then ducked under the ledge to rest and shivered against the breeze. He checked his iPhone but didn't have a signal. An owl as big as a man was perched on a branch just outside the cave, as the full moon broke through the treetops. He left the Indian Rock and followed the moon across another gully and climbed roots up the embankment on the opposite side and then walked along its deteriorating length for about a hundred paces before crossing a barbed wire fence.

Farther on past a smaller field, he walked around a rusted-out Ford and then entered the big field next to a pond, and nothing much grew between the pond and where he walked other than scrub and broom sage. He turned directly to the right and found the path that threaded along this border between the two sections of field, and he followed it until he came to a two-hundred-foot-wide flat space extending to where a scrubby hill sloped up to a house. He walked up the hill to a screened back door, and the dogs chained up around the side of the house started going crazy. Behind the screen the door was wood painted white with a peephole but no window. He propped the .22 on the outside of the frame and stood there listening to the small sounds coming from the house: footsteps, running water, the creak of a cabinet door, a TV droning.

He opened the screen door and knocked twice on the wooden door as the dogs kept up their racket. Nobody answered though he could see a middle-aged man through the window, sitting next to the red glow of his space heater. Jamie knocked on the door again and then immediately regretted coming as the man got up and crossed to the door and opened it. The man was a woodsy-looking guy with blue eyes and a beard, and when he said, "Can I help you?" Jamie sensed the man might have recently woken from a nap. He could still walk away from this, make an excuse and turn around, but he didn't.

"Sorry to bother you," he said, "but does Cortis Pittenger still live here?"

"Yeah, he still lives here. What can I do for you?"

"Well, this is gonna sound crazy, but I'm gonna tell you something so—as much as I can, anyway—so you can, uh... understand." He was just making noise and he wanted to get it over with and then he started to make a case for himself: "I'm Jamie Paddock. Roy Paddock's boy."

"Oh," he said beatifically. He yelled for the dogs to shut up and then he held the door open and said, "Well, I'm Cortis's son, Dale. Come on in."

Dale turned into the kitchen and Jamie stood at the threshold and looked inside to find the house was well made with nice wood floors and new Kenmore appliances, La-Z-Boy furniture. A couple of severed deer heads hung on plaques from the walls and the place had a distinctive odor, formaldehyde mixed with animal fur.

"You want somethin' to eat or drink?" Dale said.

"Thank you, no," Jamie answered.

Dale asked him if he was the one he always read about in the *Nicholas Chronicle* and Jamie said, "I don't think so—maybe, though," and Dale said, "Jamie, you said, right?" and Jamie said, "That's right," and then Dale got a bottle of water from the refrigerator and he gestured at a chair, and he meant by this that regrettably it was time to talk about Roy, so Jamie sat down and gave him this halfway attention and he wasn't panicking because something about the whole thing momentarily replaced his panic with curiosity.

"It's a terrible shame about your daddy," Dale said. "I guess he ain't hurtin' no more, but it's a terrible shame. All I can say is, I guess he ain't hurtin'."

"So you knew him? Or of him?"

"Well, of course I knew him. How couldn't I? Given all that."

Jamie allowed a puzzled expression to touch his face.

Dale blew out a long breath. "You'd probably better talk to Dad. Did you say you wanted somethin' to drink or eat?"

"Just wait, wait, wait, wait. Are you talkin' about the same thing?"

"What thing?"

"The thing with the goat."

"I mean, I don't know what to tell you. Roy tried to steal a goat off my dad when he was a kid. I don't know, maybe I have it wrong, though. It's just a story he tells."

"Wait, so you're just repeatin' some shit you heard—"

"Boy, I'm gonna need you to keep your tone civil—"

"But he stole a goat, you're sayin'," Jamie shouted.

"Now it'd be a cowardly thing for me to beat *on a punk faggot*!"

Jamie's face relaxed almost as if he'd been expecting this. "Yeah. Wow."

Dale looked like he was making an attempt at keeping it together. "I got no beef with you. I just heard the story."

Neither said anything else until he said, "Anyway, like I say, maybe you better talk to Dad. He ain't awake but for maybe five hours outta the day. He has cancer and his intestines're all messed up, but he'll gladly tell you about it."

Jamie didn't say anything as he followed Dale through the house and a few paces down a hallway to the open door of Cortis's bedroom, and there was a smell of sickness and old age and then Dale turned on a bedside lamp and Jamie saw Cortis. He was lying on his back with a blanket drawn up to his chin and his right arm flung behind his head, and there were oxygen tubes up his nose and a catheter bag on the bed that Dale must've recently emptied. His skin was grayish blue and thin, and Jamie thought he looked very Third World–ish.

"The cancer started in his colon," Dale said. "He's been seven ways from Sunday with this damn disease. But it's in God's hands now. Anything can happen."

Jamie thought that was a strange thing to say. It seemed like only one thing was going to happen. He stepped into the room and stood beside the body, and then Dale knelt down beside the bed and whispered something in Cortis's ear and the old man came awake and said, "What time is it?" and Dale said, "Just about six. Ten of," and then Cortis rubbed his face briskly and looked at Jamie and Jamie gave him a nod but got no acknowledgment.

"Daddy," Dale said, "this is Roy Paddock's boy, Jamie."

Cortis stared at Jamie stone-faced and said, "Now you are the dead spittin' image of your daddy now," in this strained voice and Jamie just wanted him to stop.

Dale turned and left without another word.

Jamie and Cortis paused, both looking downward until it seemed they were doing just that. "What do you remember," Jamie asked him, "about my dad?"

Cortis seemed to hold his breath a minute.

"Did you one time have a goat named Steamboat?"

"Yeah. And I'll tell you somethin' else, too."

"Will you? I'm tryin' to figure out some stuff."

"I'll tell you before your daddy was your daddy he was a lyin', thievin' son of a bitch," he said, very nearly smiling at this. "I can tell you that much for goddamn sure."

Jamie had this macabre urge to crush the old man's wind-pipe.

"I caught him swingin' his dick all over private property. Stealin' Steamboat. Well, he starts cryin' and says the cause was he got his girlfriend pregnant and was gonna sell the goat 'cause he was nowhere near done driftin' and had to leave, and I told him it didn't matter where he went he'd always be the same person. Well, he still took the goat and I never did call the police and now here you are, so who the hell cares?"

"But if—"

"Believe what you want, son, but try to keep clear of all the bullshit. What I'm sayin' is I know how it runs for guys like your daddy generally in life and I wouldn't be surprised if he wasn't up and runnin' somewhere out there."

"My dad wouldn't run out on my mom and sister," Jamie said, feeling like someone had punched him in the chest, be-cause the idea had crossed their minds, hadn't it?

"Put it this way. He almost did." Cortis pointed his gnarled fingers. "So, your daddy stands there in the barn, I mean he stands there like somebody who's been *waitin'* to stand there, weight of the world on his shoulders, and he starts talkin', and he says, 'These things, they come to me sometimes and they don't make me feel too good.' He said he never stopped hurtin'. Said he felt like somethin' in one-a them old Tarzan movies."

"Quicksand," Jamie said. "He always said that about West Virginia."

"Now none-a that shit. Have a funeral, say some prayers, but don't say it was this place that had somethin' to do with it." Cortis kept silent a minute. "People like you are always lookin' for somethin'. But you never find it here. You think this place's got some secret an' you take it personal and can't find it so you leave. You think it's holdin' some secret from you. But there ain't no goddamn secrets—it's just this goddamn burnin'— oh, Jesus, forgive me for cussin'. First I can't piss by myself no more. Gotta yell for Dale evertime. Now this."

"Whatever happened to Steamboat?" Jamie said.

Cortis thought about it. "Now that I've never knowed. I imagine he's still out there somewhere, smiling widely behind the Devil's veil and whippin' horseflies with his tail."

Cortis talked awhile longer about all sorts of things.

"It's nothin' but memories," he said. "Best left forgot."

Jamie waited for him to say more and finally he did.

"I don't know. I'd like to believe we go somewhere, but I don't know. I think it's because we're just empty .22 shells. We get far'd off and then we hit the ground."

He closed his eyes and they both got quiet.

He said, "I'm tired."

And then Dale returned and showed Jamie out like an usher at church.

It was dark and dumping snow by the time Jamie got the .22 and headed home.

He retraced his steps in the deep snow and felt like he needed something else fast, a bolt of lightning, a quick and painless change, a drug. After a while it was clear he'd gone farther into the woods than he needed. Everywhere he turned there were unfamiliar trees and branches confusing his path and it was quiet, no sign of anything, and with a growing sense of disorientation he broke into a run through the trees. The snow came harder and he couldn't see but for a foot in front of him. He stumbled along the crumbled ribbon of an old railroad track and followed it around the gully until it ended in mountain laurel shrubs twice as tall as him, and then he saw a fine twelve-pointer with a ride rack staring back at him from inside the laurel. He raised the .22 and remembered what his father had told him (*Aim for the right front shoulder. Don't shoot it in the head.*) and cocked back the hammer and put the bead on the buck's shoulder and pulled the trigger, and the beast shuddered and fell over. It was quivering as he ran over, and he pressed his knees against the body and took out his pocket-knife and killed it quickly—blade angled across its throat, near the jaw—sawing through the windpipe and bones of the neck through to the spine, and he grabbed its ankles with shaking hands and dragged it through the woods into the gully until he hit a deer path, which he followed to the creek. He was wheezing and panting as he dragged the carcass, and not an hour later he was back behind the old woodshed, and he took off his coat and set it on the picnic table and hung the buck to bleed and, with his skinning knife, opened it from crotch to jaw and threw its heap of skin and fur onto the ground and the entrails onto the woodpile. He dressed it like he'd been taught and, covered in its viscera, took the meat inside and put it in the freezer.

IT WAS EIGHT A.M. on New Year's Eve and Jamie woke in the spare bedroom having no idea where he was. He'd slept long and pleasurably and his whole body felt good, and he took a quick hot shower and then he went into the kitchen and saw a pot of coffee that he didn't drink from because he was just noticing how *off* everything smelled, like rotten food. Over and over again, he recalled his conversation with Cortis and tried to get the whole incident straightened out in his head, but something was wrong. He was troubled by a peculiar impulse to fight, which was unfamiliar but not unpleasant, and wondered if there'd ever been a choice connected with his coming back to West Virginia. He hadn't refused to come, which he thought was significant, and then he stared at his own face reflected in the glass of the coffeepot. He looked at his iPhone and saw that he had a number of texts from Sara, a number that was a bit scary, containing things that held more meaning than he was capable of understanding at the time:

"Nature is random as random we define it. It's all absurd behavior."

"Not the idea of being here or there. But being in both places at once. My veins feel weird again but you made my night the other day. You are so important to my life. You have saved me time & again. I won't be able to sleep I don't think. I'm imagining you writing songs about me. Ha. I am still awake. Guess once my phone dies I will go to slee."

And then later:

"Couldn't shower. I tried and squirmed and felt sick."

"Afraid of catching the maggots. My dad had growing under his toes."

"I am naked in bed thinking of you reading to me."

Later still:

"I'm drinking Miller Lite in an old Red Wings sweatshirt & a pair of yoga pants that make my ass look all kinds of good that it isn't."

"I really want a cigarette but I accidentally bought regular menthol instead of lights and somehow those are just too much for me."

Jamie frowned and then clicked the phone off because he couldn't tell if she was really as upset as she appeared to be or just extremely crazy, which he felt bad about.

At this precise moment, Janice began calling his name from her bedroom, and he went in and she was in bed, breathing heavily, and her face was red like it was burning, and she was rationalizing, "Nobody coulda saved your daddy."

He made a calming motion with his hand and said, "You're confused, Mommy—you're havin' a dream," and then she was struggling with the blankets, absurdly, with a pleading look of terror in her eyes, and he saw her hair and neck were wet and the blankets were wet and the sheets had taken on a sepia tinge and there was an odor like spoiled milk. He stared at the stained sheets—at their truth—and the smell of her piss was choking him and he was saying sentences that didn't mean anything. There was no reaction on her face, nothing, and this went on for a while, five or ten minutes, before he was able to get her out of bed. He yelled for Carol but got no response, and then he led Janice outside and was helping her down the porch as she feebly reached out a hand to steady herself. They got in the Jeep and drove out to Raleigh General by going around the gorge, through rusted houses with yards laid out to look like working farms and the yards were full of frozen ponds. Occasionally the road ran past formless slabs of concrete where half-finished buildings had been stalled and left to crumble, and more and more he thought the countryside was beginning to resemble something Third World–ish. They passed a yard with a dog and children playing, and Janice turned in her seat and looked with longing at them until they were out of sight. They arrived at the hospital at ten thirty and he helped Janice inside through the automatic doors of the entrance, and then he saw all the doughy Medicaid people sitting in the waiting room with their oxygen tanks. He found Janice a seat and then went to the check-in counter and said, "Janice Paddock," and the nurse, with a slight speech impediment, asked for insurance cards, so he got them from Janice's purse and brought them back. He signed her name and something about the scene troubled him, although he couldn't quite reason what it was. The nurse started humming to herself, and he walked outside and lit a cigarette in the sky's sickly light.

After half an hour, she was triaged and they sat watching Fox News on the TV. The blond anchor was doing a story on mortgages and forty-five-year-olds hustling for cashier jobs at Walmart, repossessed minivans and under-the-table grocery money, prices shooting up, the dollar crashing—all of which had befallen us because of Barack Obama.

"Things are fallin' apart," Janice said. "And nobody's actin' like they are."

Disproportionately angry, he said, "Mom, stop watchin' this bullshit."

"Well, I know what's gonna happen."

"Well, what's gonna happen then?"

"Just things. Things comin' our way."

Later, the door opened and in walked an Indian doctor with a name tag pinned to his lapel—BABHULKAR PRASAD, MD—a slight man, five-foot-five, with narrow shoulders and a bald shaven head to which he'd applied some kind of wax. "Hi, how are you this morning?" he said.

"Oh, I'm doin' all right," Janice said. "This is my son, Jamie."

Dr. Prasad shook Jamie's hand and smiled involuntarily and then said, "Nice to meet you," genuinely, and Jamie detected in the doctor's speech a foreign accent—if not exactly an Indian one, at least one of an immigrant family and newer to the country than his own.

"So I understand we had a little spell this morning?" Dr. Prasad said.

"I was just tired," she said. "I don't know if I'd call it a spell."

Dr. Prasad defined her lack of progress in a brief series of reflex tests. He asked if she'd suffered from depression "or anything like that," and she said, "No, I've been pretty good," to which he added, "Are you lethargic?" and she said, "Yeah, but—"

"Seizures?"

She shook her head. "No."

"And are you currently taking medication for anxiety, bipolar disorder, depression, schizophrenia, anything like that?"

"All I take is"—she paused—"well, I'm out, but—Copaxone."

Dr. Prasad knelt in front of her and took her left knee in his hands and drew it slowly upward and then did the same with her right knee, frowning, and if Janice was trying to resist, it was evident only from a slight trembling in her legs.

"You need to do much more stretching." He stood up and wrote something in a notepad and said, "The Copaxone working?" and then, half jokingly, "Ever think about moving some-where warmer? Maybe the beach?"

She laughed. "No, I don't think I'll ever move."

"You'll have to get yourself out," Dr. Prasad said. "With any degenerative disease there is a physical process—you know that—but just as important, we should not forget that there is a psychological process as well. Any trouble with mem-ory or anything like that?"

She said, "I don't think," and looked at Jamie with a fearful stare that worried him, and he thought, *Isn't this typical, the poor Appalachian people, the poor, dirty Appalachians with their illnesses and their poisoned land, the subspecies of American culture, eating at Applebee's and getting pregnant by their close relatives. They're fatter and sadder and dumber than everyone else, but they just can't leave the place that's making them that way.*

Dr. Prasad said she was probably experiencing an exacer-bation and that she'd need to stay in the hospital for a couple of days until they figured out the treatment. He turned to Jamie and made small talk: "Home for the holidays, helping out a little bit?" And Jamie talked with him about living in New York and being a writer and he was suddenly aware that he might've been less friendly had the doctor been white.

Janice said she wanted an eggs-in-the-basket sandwich from Cracker Barrel, so he took the Jeep and drove down the road to Cracker Barrel. Inside, they were playing a Johnny Cash song, or maybe it was Willie Nelson, and there were a lot of nostalgia products for sale. The girl standing behind the po-dium was maybe nineteen, twenty—blond, pale, unremark-able—and he said he wanted to place an order and she sent him to the checkout counter, where he paid the cashier seven or eight dollars for the eggs-in-the-basket sandwich. She said it'd be about a fifteen-minute wait. He walked around and the place was packed with fat people looking indifferent or sick, eating breakfast, all of them or at least most of them staring at him, and some people even seemed to recognize him, and then for a moment the slight weirdness he felt turned into a sort of paranoia. He picked up a magazine about West Virginia and struck a few notes on a toy piano, and then he saw Jen from the gallery standing in the corner and figured she must've lived close by and that was why she was standing alone, like him, and he walked over to her.

"Hey," he said, "I thought that was you."

"Oh, hey," she said, smiling, "good to see you. What're you doing here?"

"Oh, you know. Just... enjoying Cracker Barrel?"

She was wearing a sweater that looked like an ACE bandage and he thought it made her look very futuristic, like someone from the "real world" in *The Matrix*.

"How did everything go with... ?" she asked, looking serious.

He paused and then said, "OK, fine," and looked down. "Yeah, there was a lot going on, but I definitely got somewhere. I mean, I either got somewhere or I made myself get there. I mean, everything just flipped, y'know? The guy I thought he was, uh, I don't know."

"So do you think you got there or made yourself get there?"

"Not sure there's a difference." There was a pause. "OK, so the guy, Cortis, I went to visit him, and he told me all this stuff. Well, the weird thing is is that he sort of suggested my dad might've just run off or something. Other than that I don't know. I think about it and... what if he's right? I mean, the body is still missing."

"Oh, gosh," she said, pausing with such a comical awkwardness that it seemed like a parody of something. "That's, um, so—I don't know. You don't have to tell me."

"No, no—I want to. Hey, you feel like Cracker Barrel? To eat. Tell me you're hungry."

"No, I actually just ate—I mean, it's work, you know."

"OK, all right. I mean, like, would you like to do something? I'd like to talk to you more. We can get some dinner or maybe a coffee afterward? I thought we could go."

She blushed and said, "That'd be great. If you want."

"You want to?"

She blushed once more and said, "Sure."

They decided on a place—Secret Sandwich Society in Fayetteville—and they agreed to meet there even though he had no real idea where exactly Secret Sandwich Society was, so she took out her iPhone and showed him a couple of pictures.

"That's so nice," he said. "Anyway, seriously, meet me at eight?"

"OK," she said, grinning. "All right, I will."

Sometime later he drove back to Raleigh General and thought about Jen and her big grin, and he dreamed of what it would take to make her so happy that he could see it forever.

In the same space of time he received several more texts from Sara:

"We are all indebted to what we build ourselves from always remember that."

"I think of all the coke I said I didn't want to do anymore but at this moment any drug sounds good."

"My dad is dying. I need you, Panther."

Jamie texted, "What's going on with your dad? Are you OK?"

"I'm always OK."

"Are you sure?"

"Yes."

"Absolutely sure?"

"Nothing is absolute but at least the search for it is not just cumming in your friends' faces & hoping they'll be grateful for the pink eye you've given them."

"Jesus," Jamie said, locking his iPhone.

He went up to Janice's room. His mother was flat on her back on the hospital bed. Jamie gave her the eggs-in-the-basket sandwich, which she picked at for about forty minutes. The TV was on and Sean Hannity was talking to another Fox News personality and the sound was turned down low so he could only imagine what the two were saying to each other, and Janice didn't say anything for a long time and when she did it was in a low voice that he could barely hear, and he leaned in closer and she mumbled something and he had to ask her what she'd said and she said it again, her voice all wobbly and far off: "I like bridges. I like the way they connect two different things."

"Yeah," he said, not understanding where she was coming from.

"They don't bring things closer, but they make things feel closer. Yep, I like bridges. I ever tell you about when your Paw-Paw took us to the edge of New River Gorge Bridge?"

"Don't think so," he half whispered, trying to remember his granddad's face.

"When they first built it. It was weird to have them buildin' a big bridge just up the road. Your Paw-Paw drove us kids out to the edge of it. We got out of the car and walked to the edge. It was fun, to come to the edge. Nothin' but space. Until I got about halfway. It was nine hundred feet high and I sat at the edge and wondered if I'd ever cross it. Bein' a kid is funny, I guess. Don't remember what I thought about while I was looking over the edge. I do remember lookin' to the ground on the opposite side and seein' the big shadow of the end on the other side."

He was 99 percent sure she was about to cry. "You OK?"

"I'm just tired. I just want everything to be over. I can't take it anymore."

"It's been a hard day." He stopped and dramatically, in a low voice, said, "You should think about what the doctor said. About moving somewhere easier to get around."

"That doctor just needs to mind his own business."

"That's what he does. He's the doctor—"

"Then he came to the wrong country. He can go back to India."

He shook his head uselessly and sighed.

"Your daddy wouldn't've wanted to move. He never could leave this place."

"Mom, if you don't move somewhere more practical…"

Without making any sign of protest, without even glancing at him, she put the sandwich down and then folded her arms. "When are you goin' back?" she asked.

"Tomorrow. Since there's nothing happening with Dad, I should get back."

"Well."

He turned to the TV and took a lingering look at the conservative talk show going on and then turned away and rubbed his eyes. "You don't think we'll get any answers about Dad, do you?" he said. "About why he did what he did."

"Maybe not," she said. "And I think that might be just as well."

"How much more do you know about this goat he had?"

"Your daddy had all kinds of animals—I guess you forgot that."

"You didn't think I'd find it enlightening that he stole the goat? Or funny at least?"

Janice was frozen, her fearless presence seeming to dull upon hearing this. She stared at Jamie and he stared back hatefully. "You think you know it all," she said.

"There's somethin' you're not telling me." He looked at her and saw how tired she was and his anger became fuzzy around the edges. "Well, that's fine because I don't care. I have my own problems," he said. "I'm just trying to get to know him. That's all."

JAMIE PUSHED whatever guilty thoughts he had out of his mind and left the hospital and drove back to Mount Lookout through the flurries of snow, and when he pulled into the driveway he saw Carol down at the woodpile. She was skinning what he assumed was a deer and he got out of the Jeep and walked down there, and as he approached her she looked at him with such dubiety that he felt like a stranger cast in the image of some monster that kills travelers who pass through its land. He said, "Mom's in the hospital; where were you this morning?" and she said, "Is she really? Is she OK? What happened?" and he said, "Yeah, she's all right, but—"

And then he saw it: what he'd assumed was a deer was actually this big dead dog, one that'd probably, he thought, been run over by a car. The maggots and buzzards had been at it, and there were ropes of saliva hanging from its mouth and blood and bits of its skull speckled the grass, and he looked at the open eyes and for a second it looked to him like it'd seen what'd come for it but that what it'd truly seen had been too powerful for its imagination. It didn't depress him, just made him feel weird, and he couldn't say anything for a beat, only stare at those eyes and wonder what they'd seen.

"The hell you doin' cuttin' up roadkill?"

"Cleaned 'im up a bit. Been a thin herd this year, the deer, I mean. The winter, I guess. You ain't seen it, bein' away, but ask anybody around here. Times're tough."

"What're you doin' with this? Are you eatin' it?"

She didn't say anything.

"This is roadkill," he said. "You're not eating it?"

"Yeah," she said, but she was nervous, constantly looking around.

"Carol, tell me what you're doin' with this."

She looked sad, like there was something on her mind, and he couldn't understand why she didn't comprehend that he wanted to be closer to her, that he cared about her.

"There's nothin' to tell."

"I mean, what's goin' on?"

"Stop askin' me *questions*!"

"What's goin' on?" he asked again, trying to elicit some feeling.

He could feel she was tense and knew it was the tenseness of someone who was about to tell a secret and then she moaned softly. "I been—I been sellin' it to these black people up the road. Four months now. Everbody in this town's been into stuff like that for the money. That ain't nothin' special. You get in a bind money-wise and you think of all the ways to get out, that's all. It's just natural. Besides, they'd eat sawdust if you put it in their palm."

He looked at her and thought, *No way, oh, no way,* and it felt like one of those moments when the rug is pulled out from under you, like when you hear the song "Higher and Higher" start playing and you expect it to be Jackie Wilson's voice but then it turns out to be that shitty Rod Stewart version and it's so nauseating that the air around you starts shaking.

"There're two kinds of people in this world: those that take and the ones they take from. When ya gonna see we were born on the wrong side of that line bein' born here and all?"

"Bullshit. There never was a disability check, was there? You aren't gettin' money from disability." It sounded clinical and unemotional. "I'm such a fuckin' idiot."

"We needed that money! Things're different since you left—"

"No," he said, like he was talking to a child, "no, Carol, no, we don't do this," and then he watched her hand ball into a fist and she hit him in the face with it and she was about to do it again but he grabbed her wrist before she could. "Don't hit me again," he said, trying to sound angry. "If you do I'll just hit you right back. Do you understand that?"

"You think you're better than everbody else. You don't see this, but I see it: it's what that city did to you. You let that city get the better of you since you moved up there."

"The city didn't do anything to me," he said. "It was this place."

She shut her eyes tightly and shook her head back and forth.

"Mom doesn't know about this, does she? Did Dad know?"

There was a pause that felt like it might've been the longest pause of his life, and then she gave him this look—slight, hopeless—and she said he'd been doing it to the same family for years. If she was telling the truth, what his father had done was terrible, but it was what he'd had to do. And it proved, even if it didn't excuse, the lengths that hungry people in the mountains would go to. He missed the old days and wanted them back so badly, and then he realized that Carol probably felt the same way and he tried to think of something, anything, to say, hoping a shred of sympathy would break through to her. He turned to her and said, raising his voice at first, then letting it drop softer, "Killed a deer the other night. Meat's in the freezer."

THEY GOT THE PACKS of deer meat from the freezer and drove up the road to the black people's house. He thought about Sara and then he took out his iPhone and opened her text conversation and typed, "did u find a place to stay?" but then backspaced it so she wouldn't see the animated ellipses that indicated he was typing. He looked out the window and it was quiet and it'd stopped snowing and the day was clear and the mountains at all points of the horizon glowed blue, but far above them dark, low clouds approached, discoloring the surface of the fields. It was beautiful and distant, like a postcard of heaven. He looked at it and understood what his father had meant when he'd said a person could get to hate that view. He understood how much he wanted to let go of it, how much he wanted it to let go of him. And after looking at it some more, how much he wanted to light a match and just blow the whole fucking thing to hell. After looking at it some more it seemed like a really fun idea and not a hard thing to do.

The black people's house sat on this half-acre lot a couple of miles up the road and looked like a bizarro *Brady Bunch* house: single-wide, vinyl siding, and a renovation at some point that had added a wraparound porch to the left side. The front yard looked so neglected Jamie wondered if anyone cared about presentation anymore. The grass was patchy and uncut, and the old spruce trees standing by the property line had lost all their needles and now were just huge gray triangles, and the mailbox was made of aluminum and rusted and read PERKINS. He grabbed the packs of frozen deer meat and followed Carol across the yard to the front porch, where an old black man was sitting on a porch swing, eating a can of Pringles and not wearing a coat.

"Well, there's Miss Carol," the black man said. His voice was idle with a pleasant drawl; it was unmistakably West Virginian, but smooth, like a stream of water from a tap.

Carol said, "Hel-lo," spoken low with an exclamation, and the man said, "You get yourself a deer or somethin'?" and she said, "Sure did," reluctantly. Jamie started feeling self-conscious and then Carol introduced him and he took off his sunglasses and said, "Nice to meet you," and the man, who introduced himself as Derrick, looked him over dubiously before saying, "Nice to meet you, too," and then he took the packs of deer meat with his grease-stained hands and said, "Well, come on in."

They followed Derrick inside and there was a thin veneer of cigarette smoke in the air and Jamie stood there, too nervous to say anything. The house looked like old people lived there. There were romance novels (had to be a hundred older paperbacks) piled up on an end table and strange rubber-glove turkeys hanging from wires on the windowsill, and the washer and dryer were behind the couch, which he thought was odd, and the dryer was running so it made the hair on the back of his neck sort of damp. There was a big flat-screen TV tuned to a crime channel and the host's beautiful voice was talking about death and the volume was up to like forty, but he didn't want to do anything wrong, so he didn't turn down the volume.

Carol inspected the rubber-glove turkeys. "You seem like you're keepin' busy."

"Busy? Only thing I can do is watch the grass grow an' the tadpoles fuck," Derrick said, walking over to the window and opening it, waving the cigarette smoke out. "Mimi," he said, "get out here an' see Carol. She brought deer meat. Better'n seven pounds."

There was the sound of footsteps and then an old black woman, Mimi, Jamie presumed, came into the living room drying her hands on a dishrag. There was something pleasant about the woman's appearance—she had a good smile, what people called a "genuine smile"—and she smelled like garlic and was tastefully dressed in a Christmas-themed sweater and jeans.

"Well, this is unexpected," she said. "How you doin', honey?"

"Oh, pretty good," Carol said. "How about you? You have a good Christmas?"

Mimi hugged Carol without seeming to notice or care that she didn't hug back, and then Mimi put her hand to her throat and stared at Jamie and looked totally stunned.

"Oh," Mimi managed to say. "I'm sorry. You look just like your dad standin' there. I just thought that was your dad. You must be Carol's brother, Jamie," she said, friendly as hell.

"That's what I was about to say, he does look like him," Derrick said.

"Your house is very nice," Jamie said, and he felt so stupid that he couldn't come up with a cleverer thing to say. For some reason in that moment he wanted to be like a Kardashian on a reality show, being fed expertly written lines, and even though he knew the Kardashians were morons, that didn't stop him from wanting to be as clever as they were on TV. He thought that was why Americans had given up on real life and why everyone was living in some false reality of their own delusions, like *The Matrix*.

"It's miserable in the summer," Mimi said, her face twisted with mock loathing. "Gets hot like you wouldn't believe. But it's pretty. I love this house here. Have for thirty years."

"They brought us some deer meat," Derrick said, "better'n six or seven pounds." He took a wadded-up roll of moist bills from his pocket and counted. "How much for?"

Carol's eyes turned thoughtful as she studied the bills. "Keep it. Merry Christmas."

"You sure?" Derrick said.

"Give her some money," Mimi said.

"No, no, really," Carol said. "We got a whole freezer full."

"You wanna sit down? I be able to talk you all into some sloppy joes?" Mimi said.

"I gotta get home and start cookin'," Carol lied. "We gotta get goin' back home."

"Now you can stay for a sloppy joe, can't you? We have so much extra."

They all went into the kitchen and Mimi took a Rubbermaid container of premade hamburger meat from the fridge and started frying it on the stove, and then Derrick filled a crud-crusted glass with orange tap water and handed it to Jamie and Jamie drank it and looked at Carol, and Carol was staring at the sizzling sloppy joe meat in the pan. The attention this new family was pushing his way made him start ignoring certain things, especially the way Carol's eyes widened as they were staring at the sloppy joe meat, but also things like how he didn't know his real family anymore. He was answering questions about living in New York and going to NYU and writing, and no one gave him a weird attitude.

"So big and away at the city," Mimi said, and Jamie felt an awkward closeness with them.

"How did you know our dad?" he said.

Derrick said, "He was gettin' Carol a Nintendo for Christmas, oh, about five, six years ago, and we was waitin' in line together. Stayed from morning till it was dark and talked all the time about nothin'. He was better'n that. Better'n what he did."

Mimi stirred the sloppy joe mixture into the reddish-brown meat and then ladled out a cup of melted fat and grease. Derrick said his own daddy had been a bastard.

"Made us kids walk to Beckley to look for a job," he said. "Who does that? I didn't know he was such a bastard till later on. He got that way livin' in a six-foot-by-five-foot tent durin' that Depression and he didn't believe in God. He said, 'How can I believe in a god that puts me down in that reformatory down in Cabin Creek and work me fifteen hours a day?' and Mama said, 'Because you had three square meals a day and water to drink.' She said she told him because God told her to tell him and she told him the very next day. That's just how it is. Everbody thinks you can make your own world. Fact is, you can't. You gotta live in the world the way it is. You gotta live in it the way it is or find another world, y'hear?"

"Why didn't you leave?" Jamie said.

"Leave for where? You can leave for wherever you want to, but this place?" He gestured around to his house falling apart. "You know." He paused. "This place is like a shadow that ain't never gone an' I can't see that it ever will be. Got coal dust in my lungs. All those years minin' it, breathin' in that poison. It's there forever, a part of me. It's like that."

Yeah. It's like that.

They sat at the dining table in the kitchen and spooned the sloppy joe mix onto hamburger buns from Walmart, and Derrick and Mimi started eating theirs and Jamie stared at his before finally taking a bite (it had a ton of garlic in it but tasted all right) and Carol just stared at hers on the plate. Derrick and Mimi were in a heavy conversation about how another of their neighbors had sold a few acres of land to a coal company, which meant their land would be stripped, and Jamie was saying "uh-huh" in differing variations.

"Goddamn people are blatant ignorant around here," Derrick said.

"Last I heard," Mimi said, "they were sellin' it to start a landscapin' business over in Raleigh County. He'd come down and do the Riddles' lawn on occasion."

"Likely he ain't even got a lawn by now," Derrick said.

Jamie said, "Uh-huh," and then he noticed Carol hadn't touched her sloppy joe and she looked over at him and her eyes acknowledged his and he knew it wasn't good. He finished off his sloppy joe even though he knew it was probably made with roadkill meat, and then he leaned back with this big, deflated sigh. "Well, I guess we should get goin'," he said.

"Do me a favor, Jamie," Derrick said, standing up and taking a couple of plates with him over to the sink. "Eat that last sloppy joe for me. Don't want it to go to waste."

"Oh, no thanks," he said, "I'm good. I do appreciate it, though."

"Big guy like you can't polish off one more little sloppy joe?"

Patting his stomach. Mock exhaustion. "'Fraid not."

"Well, Carol, you aim to eat any of yours at all?"

"I have to tell you all somethin'," she said, glancing sideways, and then she couldn't help it—she took a deep breath and all in a rush said, "You're eatin' roadkill."

There was an empty silence, and while this revelation was disgusting in its own right, it was something Jamie was equipped to deal with.

"Come on, Carol," he said, laughing, "stop kiddin' around."

He took out his iPhone and texted her as though this message would somehow get through: "please, we'll talk later."

"No, I'm serious," Carol said, almost pleadingly, as she kept glancing around, and Jamie just wanted her to stop but he also didn't want her to look at him.

"What are you talkin' about?" Mimi said. "That's perverted and disgusting."

"I don't care," Carol said. "How bad am I for sayin' that? But I don't. I just wanted you to know. It wasn't deer meat. It wasn't deer meat all along. Today's is, though."

The conversation was on the verge of becoming a fight. Jamie could hear his heart pounding in his ears. He could feel it in his throat and his fingertips quivered. He looked at Carol and his face was like *please don't do this* and he wanted to say he was sorry, sorry about Will and the party, sorry he'd hurt her in some way he didn't fully understand, sorry he'd left everyone behind. He wanted to say he loved her, but he knew the chance to say it was in the past. She looked at the text message, but from the way she wouldn't look at him and the hurt look in her eyes, it seemed they'd already parted in some fundamental way.

"Carol, what's goin' on?" Derrick said.

Carol sat there quietly and then she started giggling uncontrollably until her eyes watered and her face contorted in a laugh. "Nah, I'm just kiddin'." She laughed and then coughed, wiping her eyes. "It was just a joke." Her voice sounded high-pitched and somewhat scared.

No one laughed and they all sat there and ate the roadkill sloppy joes.

Jamie grabbed the last sloppy joe like he was afraid it might escape.

"I was just kiddin'," Carol said, her mouth full of sloppy joe.

And in some warped way Jamie was proud of her.

Jamie and Carol drove back to the house and the sky got unusually dark and the clouds were bulging with more "thundersnow," like the radio had said, and though this shouldn't have been a problem, he somehow knew that it was. He drove through the mountains and the radio was howling "Tarzan Boy" by Baltimora as Carol listened, rapt, and then he turned down the volume and tried to focus on the silence between the notes. They saw this old dog on the side of the road and she started laughing. "Remember Will's dog? Remember ol' Skinhead?"

He laughed and cried, "Oh god, ol' Skinhead."

"Whatever happened to that ol' dog?"

He remembered that Uncle Mike had killed the dog because it'd bitten a chunk out of Will's leg, and Jamie had what seemed to him an intense desire to tell her but found himself unable to do so, recalling the days when they'd all played with the dog in the yard.

His iPhone buzzed and Carol looked at the screen.

"Says it's somebody named Sara." She opened the messages app and then read the text message with a speculative pause between each word. "'I am about in fuck-ing tears,'" she read. "It says, 'bc I'm at the Laundromat but all I have is Starbucks money not real money and I don't know how-to-act-like-a goddamn add-ult and all I want to do is choke on your—'" She stopped midsentence, scandalized. "This your girlfriend or somethin'?"

"Somethin' outta the blue," he said, eyes down.

"You still like livin' in New York?"

"Sure, I guess I do."

"Well, it sure as hell makes my world seem bigger." She laughed.

He looked at her and smiled sadly. "It's kind of like," he started, "you ever get that feeling you stepped into the wrong life?"

He ignored the eyes telling him, *No, I don't get that feeling, you idiot; this is the only life I could possibly imagine.* He ignored them and kept talking: "You keep telling yourself, *This can't be right, this isn't me. I musta walked through the wrong door.* Like you're standing in the bathroom and looking in the mirror and you can't even count how many faces are in there anymore. And you know this just isn't who you are. But you keep wearin' all these faces like you're some kind of master of disguise. And the worst part of it is you realize you're actually pretty fucking good at it." There was a longish silence during which he tried to figure out what to say. "Funny thing is," he continued, "talking to you like this has probably been one of the only good parts of my life lately."

More silence, pregnant and vaguely angry feeling.

"I've been meaning to ask," he said. "Are you doing all right after the other night?"

"You never asked me how I was doin' before."

"Well," he said, "I'm not gonna let things like this happen to you again. Things like Will and roadkill. That's what I've been thinkin'. I'm gonna come home more often."

"I can take care of myself."

He looked at her, genuinely confused. "I didn't say you couldn't."

"Just shut up and let me deal with it. Can you do that? Are you capable of doin' that?"

He could only stare at her with this big, hurt *what?* expression.

"It's like you got two of you in there and they're fightin' it out tryin' ta figure out which one is gonna win. But your whole life was just an arrow headed away from this place. And there's no turnin' back. It's great, but it's a one-way ticket. You can't help me now."

He stared out the window. "You're my sister. I love you."

"I believe you," she said. "But sometimes I don't even know who you are. And the thing that really breaks my heart? I hate you, too. I hate you. More than anyone I ever knew."

He was surprised and she turned her head away so her face was just a blur. He checked himself in the rearview mirror to see what she was talking about. He could've used a shower and a shave and a good night's sleep, but other than that he was still him.

"I'm sorry," he murmured. It was all he could think to say.

WHEN THEY GOT BACK to the house, they didn't say anything to each other and Jamie turned the TV to CNN and the daytime anchor was talking about a serial killer in New York City and his "pattern of killing," and how he was "probably an escaped mental patient" because his "spiral of depersonalization had gone so deep" that he'd "reversed the Nietzschean process" and "reverted from a civilized animal" (*"Civilized animal"—what a strange choice of phrase,* Jamie thought idly) to a "rough imitation of a human being," and after sitting there on separate sides of the couch for what might've been fifteen minutes, Carol said she was going to the hospital to see Janice and then she put on her coat and left. Jamie turned off the TV and sat there in silence before going into the bathroom and staring at himself in the mirror for forty-five seconds, imagining what he might look like on the cover of *Time* one day.

He went into his parents' bedroom and started digging through his father's dresser again, hoping to find some clue that he was alive. His father's Social Security card was in there. Titles to vehicles. Nothing special. Nothing that carried any kind of message or solved any mysteries. Just shit his father had collected throughout his entire life. Searching the documentation, a horrible thought struck him: What if his family, the people who had lived with his dad until the very day he died, were in reality strangers in their own home? What if they truly knew nothing? They didn't know a damn thing about Roy, what he liked, what he hated, what his dreams were. They thought he was only what he was to them: a simple guy who dug around in the dirt. Not the smartest, not an English or math guy, but at least he wasn't a pillhead or a welfare abuser like a lot of guys were those days.

Jamie thought about what Carol had said earlier, about two souls fighting it out, trying to figure out which would win. Well, about that second, secret soul that belonged to their dad—the one that stole the goat, the one that was in pain, the artist—they knew nothing at all. But, when you think about it, that's kind of the point of living in the mountains, isn't it? To remain strangers. To tell society to go fuck itself. To keep your distance and avert your eyes and keep your secrets. Da Vinci was almost the first person to see mountains not as an obstacle but rather as an opportunity, and he looked crazy doing it, which tells you the kind of person it takes to overcome mountains and make them a home. Maybe this was the reason the place aroused in Jamie such a passion. The distance, the secrets. The fact that he and his family were so fucking *good* at it all.

He still had several hours before he had to meet Jen, so he watched an episode of *Twin Peaks* on Netflix. It was one of the ones with Heather Graham, and even though his favorite character had always been Audrey, there was just something about Annie now that he thought about it. He noticed she actually had tits and her red lips were parted and she was just a little wiser, and a flash of blood went straight to his cock and he adjusted himself in his jeans and wasn't planning on doing more than just touching himself, but then he gripped tighter and stroked faster and he went into the bathroom and didn't stop until he jerked off into a wad of toilet paper and then he flushed the wad down the toilet, dripping with his come.

After taking some ibuprofen and drinking a bottle of water, he put on his coat and grabbed his father's .22 and went back into the woods. The snow was still around three inches deep, and he followed the deer path out of the mountain laurel and saw quite a few deer tracks, little raccoon handprints, and bird traces. He walked to the opposite side of the mountain, to a cluster of trees on a plateau where Uncle Mike had put a tree stand many years prior, and then he found the tree stand and climbed up the ladder. The view was good and he could see the deer path coming out of the oaks below him that led to the creek, and it was about that time of day when the animals would be heading back up to the high ground where they'd pass the night. He sat there in the tree stand and held Steamboat the Goat in his palm.

It was late in the afternoon when he heard movement in the brush, and then he looked down from the tree stand and saw Will coming out of the pine cover about thirty yards away, wearing a camo suit and dopey orange hat, and Jamie thought, *He looks like a fucking redneck wearing a camo suit and dopey orange hat*. And then he took the .22 off safety and held his breath and watched, fascinated, as Will got closer, and then he lifted the barrel of the .22 and put his finger on the trigger and traced the movement of Will's skull.

This is not fiction, not one of the stories he reads in Brooklyn. This is him murdering his cousin Will.

But why?

For what he'd done to Carol?

No.

Well, sort of. But more.

For *who he was*?

Yes. That was it.

If life was a terrifying series of "previously on" smash cuts, then this was the one right before the scene cut to black with a dramatic thud. He thought about the life he'd left behind in West Virginia, who he was, what he wanted, the shadows cast across his life by his father's death, and he realized if the stand hadn't been placed so high Will might've seen him, and then he realized if Will saw him then he'd be the dead one and he'd ascend to heaven, and he imagined being welcomed into heaven by the Backstreet Boys and they'd all be wearing white like they did in that one video and they'd sing, "You're finally free."

It was beautiful and he was tempted to shoot and miss on purpose.

But he didn't and Will passed under the tree stand without seeing him, and Jamie waited until he'd gone far enough down the hill and then he flipped the safety on the .22 and quietly descended the ladder. He watched Will walk away and he felt kind of scared and found the silence unbearable so he shouted the only thing he could think of, which was "Hey," and then he hoped to god that Will didn't hear him, but then Will turned around, confused, touching his gun, and said, "Jesus. You scared the shit outta me."

Jamie tried to think of something tough to say, but he just laughed.

"You tryin' to get yourself a deer?" Will said. "What're you huntin' with?"

"Twenty-two."

"This here's my baby. Winchester. Got the beavertail forearm an everthing."

Jamie stared straight ahead. "That's real nice."

There was an obvious silence that lasted forever.

"Hey, I just wanted to say I'm sorry for the other night," Will said.

"Hey, man, I've been desperate for some pussy before, too," he blurted out. It just kind of popped out and Will frowned and then looked at him with this shit-eating grin, but as Jamie glared at him the grin disappeared and his face became a skull.

"I oughta kick your ass for what you did, motherfucker," Jamie said.

"Look, I thought she was another girl. Boo only wanted to fuck her a little. Fuckin' chimps do it to each other while they sleep. I mean, he was even gonna eat her pussy for her," he said, and then, with this bare sarcasm, "I thought maybe you'd understand that, Mr. New York."

"Is that what you want? To fuck your cousin? You fucked her, too, didn't you?"

Will looked at him like he was doing mental math. "What?"

"Yeah, don't you just love the way it feels when you go down on your cousin, when it's just you and your cousin and you wanna taste her? Don't you just love to slip your tongue inside your cousin just as she comes? Or maybe it doesn't matter which cousin?" He was talking too fast for Will to process and he could feel his face turning all red. "Maybe you'd like me to fuck you in that tight ass of yours. I mean, bone you real hard till you're clawin' up my back— Jesus, that'd be good—*and then after I fuck you hard up your ass I could put my balls in your mouth while I come all over your hillbilly face.*"

"What the fuck?"

Jamie imagined taking the braid of copper wire wrapped in pink rubber from his father that he'd left back at his apartment in the city and sodomizing Will at gunpoint with it while Will wept inconsolably, but since he didn't have the copper braid he just thought about strangling Will, but he didn't want to give Will any valid reason to put his hands on him because Will probably would've kicked his ass or arrested him.

He started walking away, promising himself that this would be the last time he'd see any of these fucking people, and he heard Will's voice:

"Where the hell are you goin', you fuckin' pussy—"

"Happy New Year!" he said too loudly.

He walked back to his parents' house the long way and stopped at Indian Rock and wished that, in the movie of his life, things had gone differently. He wished he'd punched Will or something, and then he started a fire and took the coals from the fire with his trembling hands and scrawled the word MINO-TAUR on the rock. He didn't know why or what it meant, but he stood back at a distance and looked at the giant word and thought it was beautiful.

He even took a picture of the word with his iPhone.

Where the hell are we going?

Where are we headed?

THAT NIGHT, Jamie drove to Secret Sandwich Society in Fayetteville to meet Jen. He parked the Jeep in a side parking lot that was allotted for some kind of hair stylist and then walked inside, and the place was packed with people wearing masks and it was vaguely hipster and had been redecorated to resemble someone's idea of a masquerade ball, complete with flax costumes and wildsmen, sequins, and a Walmart disco ball hanging from the ceiling. He realized it was New Year's Eve and everyone had turned to stare at him. Two waitresses stopped him at the entrance to the dining area and reminded him there was a sixty-dollar "cover," and he thought that was crazy and then he texted Jen to make sure she was coming before he paid it. He allowed himself to be stared at as he looked at the ceiling and thought about his week, and before he moved to the porch his phone vibrated and he saw it was a text from Jen that said: "be there in a few!" She arrived around ten minutes later and also seemed surprised that it was a masquerade party, and they said their hellos and then paid the sixty dollars and the waitress ushered them out onto the deck and he peered back into the dining area to see if there was anyone he recognized. The deck was cold, warmed by two giant space heaters, and the people were bundled in North Face gear but still wore masquerade masks and other aristocratic disguises.

"Should we feel stupid for not wearing masks or whatever?" Jen said, once they were seated at a table in the corner of the deck. "Should we go somewhere else?"

And then the waitress said in a singsongy voice, "There you guys go," and went back in the dining area.

"I just feel like we should've worn masks or something," Jen said.

"No, it's fine," he said. "It's nice. It seems a little... something. Like it's not a strip mall with a Walmart or other generic rural things you see around here."

"Yeah, it's different," she said, smiling. "It's nice to get out."

There was a twenty-second silence and she looked around the deck with this self-consciously worried expression. He thought what he'd said had hurt her feelings, so he looked around; noticing that the couple sitting at the table next to them looked like tourists. The man, with his tan skin, gray hair, and North Face jacket, looked like a vacationing professor, and the woman, with her Botoxed face, old-style Jennifer Aniston haircut, and North Face jacket, looked like a 1990s debutante. Jamie tried not to stare at the floor so he looked at Jen; she still seemed self-conscious and, finding the silence incriminating, he cleared his throat.

"So what'd you do over the holidays?" he said.

"I honestly just went to my mother's house and watched HGTV for twelve hours a day."

"Oh," he said, nodding in this overly enthusiastic way.

"Yeah, she ended up falling and hitting her face on the toilet seat or something, so I went over there on Christmas Eve Eve. We're not really talking right now, though—because I wanted to go out—which seems good because she's got this distorted 'obsession with control' thing going on and everything gets blown way out of proportion and"—she began to blush, and then, in the same sentence, without changing tone—"what'd you do?"

"Well..." he stalled, "it's been really weird"—he laughed—"and I don't even know why I'm here. Since a couple weeks ago, when my dad died, I knew I had to come back. I mean, actually, for a while before that. I don't know—I haven't really done much." He was kind of nervous, but their mutual silence forced him to continue. "My mom's sick and my sister..." He stopped and took a deep breath. "It's just—" Again, he stopped and he realized he was looking at her imploringly, his forehead probably creased with anxiety, and then he concluded, "Now you're probably gonna ask me a lot of questions."

"Not if you don't want me to," she said.

They stared at each other for a beat and the light from the space heaters burned over them in this warm and electric way, and then a waitress—the one who'd brought them to the table—came and lit a single candle on the table and stared at him like she wanted to fuck and he allowed it to happen but didn't reciprocate, and then she asked if they were drinking tonight in an accentless monotone and they said yes, to which she replied, "All the free champagne you can drink," and Jen brought her fingers up to her mouth and made an *ooh* sound that he thought was sexy. She ordered champagne and he started with an IPA so his lucidity wouldn't wear off, and the waitress left for two minutes before returning with their drinks.

"So when'd you graduate?" Jen said. "Oops, that's a question."

"It's OK," he said, and laughed. "I went to NYU for a couple years, but it was too expensive. Don't matter how big a scholarship looks on paper, New York's still expensive for a hillbilly."

"No, I mean, what year did you graduate high school."

"Oh," he said, "2006. I'm an old man."

"Where'd you go?"

"Nicholas County," he said hesitantly.

"What—really? I went there too."

"Are you serious?"

"Class of oh-nine."

He squinted at her. "I don't remember you," he told her, and then added, after her silence that he mistook for anger, "But I don't remember anything from 'before'"—he grinned sheepishly—"sorry."

She frowned. "Wow, 2006. You are old. Remember the two thousands?"

"No, not really," he said. "I remember everyone had those trashy highlights in their hair for some reason. Probably thanks to Kelly Clarkson, that Republican bitch."

She stared at him without blinking for a beat.

"Oh, wow, that was a joke. I shouldn't've said that," he said. "I don't know why I said that. I mean, like I had highlights in my hair when I was thirteen or something."

She was laughing hard. "Did your mom put them in for you?"

"Yeah, she did actually," he said mock defensively.

They laughed and the waitress returned and took their order. Jen looked at the menu and ordered the Churchill, which was a sandwich with Swiss, provolone, cheddar, and spinach, and he ordered the Jefferson (roast beef, horseradish mayo), another IPA, and a side salad with raspberry vinaigrette, and then the waitress left and he overheard the couple at the next table talking to a Jewish-looking guy: *"Oh yeah? What do you do?"*... *"I work with a sustainability nonprofit that can interface with an external market."*... *"Righteous."*

"So, wow, like"—Jen paused—"why'd you want to go to New York?"

He explained it in a few sentences.

"Wow, that's just so cool. So are you totally prolific or what?"

The way she said it suggested she didn't know what *prolific* meant, but he didn't care. "Well, I actually haven't written anything in weeks. I'm starting to feel like shit."

Overheard: *". . . eliminate the need for coal and provide all the cultural advantages of modern life using the bare minimum of natural resources..."*

"What, is it like writer's block or something?"

"Well, I lost something—actually it was stolen from me—this arrowhead, and I haven't really been able to do anything since. I think it's—"

"...put an old penny in your mouth and suck it. That metal tang you taste is what the water tastes like when you get close to this place."

"—magic, like Popeye's spinach. I mean, I got it back." He took the stone from his pocket and Jen's eyes lit up. "But still, something's missing, I can't quite..."

Jewish-looking guy: *"I've owned this place for five years and it's getting better—"*

Professor-looking guy: *"Is there a big divide in the community?"*

"Well," Jen said, "I'm sure you'll get back into the swing of it."

"Things are getting better, but we still get a lot of... REDNECKS."

Jamie looked over at the Jewish-looking owner, the professor-looking guy, and the debutante-looking woman, and the woman made a series of sympathetic "ohs" and Jamie couldn't tell if they were condescending or friendly, and they just kept right on talking about how "things" were getting "better" because certain "people" were "staying away" from Fayetteville and how it was "a haven"—*But for whom?* Jamie thought—and the woman kept saying "oh" in her friendly, condescending tone that was more condescending than friendly.

"You seem distracted," Jen said, looking at him worriedly.

"These people next to us are just dickheads," he whispered.

"I noticed," she said. "Yeah, I'm actually afraid of that."

"Afraid of what?"

"That I'll never leave this shithole. That I'll die here, suffering."

"Wallowing in it."

She looked at him. "Yes, wallowing in it."

They sat there in silence for a beat.

"If I had a nice house one day, I could just"—she paused—"set a bowl."

"Just set a bowl. That'd be nice. Did you ever imagine," he said, "like, a guy who was born somewhere far, far away and it felt to him like he was searching for his home his whole life and it's like if he could just *get there*, he'd *see*, y'know—because he could look back—"

He was getting emotional so he stopped and laughed to himself.

"Why don't you just leave?" he said.

"I'll probably never leave. I can't."

"You could leave. You could..."

21

WHEN THEIR FOOD ARRIVED, they both ordered more drinks and then ate and talked for another forty-five minutes or so. It was so loud in there, but by the way they were talking they might've been the only two people in the place. Jamie took a long pull from his beer bottle. Jen took a paperback I Ching, a pen, a blank sheet of paper, and three pennies from her purse.

"Where'd you learn to do this?" he asked.

"Asian studies majors get all the mystic powers," she said, rattling the pennies in her palm. "Now think of a question you want an answer to. Well, not a question—more like a direction. Like 'Direct me to a good harvest next year' or something."

All at once he thought she looked so beautiful sitting there, the light playing off her features, her hair brown and thick, her face kind, that he wanted to ask the Chinese magic if he'd ever see her again but "Where are we headed?" was all he could think of.

"I know my question," he made sure he said aloud.

She nodded and threw the coins six times and then added up their totals and drew a series of lines on the blank paper, hexagram style, in the order dictated by the I Ching book. It took about a minute and she studied the lines on the paper in a way that suggested she was going to say something about them, but the waitress came and asked if everything was all right and they said, "Yes, it's perfect," and then the waitress left.

"What does it say?" he said, referring to the hexagram.

"It says..." She paused, then squinted at it closely, rereading it. "It says, well, that you offer a balance to the world around you. Traditionally hexagram fourteen represents a great possession. Something is coming. Big change... powerful, wild... it may be a good thing... or it may possess you. Hexagram fourteen is all about stepping outside your normal world in order to gain a piece of wisdom. You literally have to be possessed by the world. Are you familiar with the first emperor of China?"

"No."

"Ying Zheng," she said, "wanted eternal life. Never got it, though. One thing or another. Conquering nearby nations. Assassination attempts. Poverty. So, what does he do?"

"Uh, he dies?"

"Oh, he dies. But before that. He unifies the Seven Kingdoms. He declares himself Qin Shi Huang, the first emperor of China. But guess what he does next."

"Gosh, I don't know."

"Strange thing," she said. "He starts drinking mercury because he thinks it will make him live forever. Then he thinks he becomes superhuman, a magnificent god. He gets his slaves and starts building himself a tomb to pass eternity in. One night, he gets a call; it's his head architect. He tells the emperor his tomb is finished. All those slaves dug that hole in the ground for ten years. So the emperor goes running outside to see it. 'It's beautiful,' he says, 'thank you.' Then he comes to this library where documents will be kept. The emperor says, 'Well, after we burn all the books, we will need ink and paper to write a new history.' Guess what the architect does. Guess! He gets an octopus to make ink. Then he gets salt water. He plants like the 'necessary trees' to make paper. Apple trees, for apples to eat. Then he gets fresh soil. Then he remembers they'll need calligraphy brushes. To make a calligraphy brush, you need bristles, so you need goats, weasels, and rabbits, right? For ten more years, the slaves dig in the cave. They hang a giant lamp from the ceiling to act as the sun. The architect brings in dirt. He diverts a river to irrigate the pastures. The slaves plant apple trees; the goats, weasels, and rabbits are bred. As soon as the architect solves one problem, a million more crop up. It becomes clear that the world is a complex thing. The architect realizes he's making an exact copy of the world, and he goes mad. For nearly forty years, the tomb is expanded until it becomes an exact copy of the world we live in. Finally, it's finished. But before the emperor inspects it, the architect looks at his creation and just starts crying, and instead of going back home, he locks himself in the tomb."

"Oh shit," Jamie said. "What happened to him?"

"He forgot the perfect world he lived in wasn't the real one. I like to think he bit into one of those fake apples and thought nothing would ever be quite as delicious."

Jamie was mildly drunk by the time dinner was over, so he offered to pay the entire check, which came to another sixty-some dollars. It was around ten o'clock and outside it was cold and there was a faint snowfall, almost like a mist, but no flakes really. He said he happened to have had a very good time and Jen said that she had, too, but that she had to get back because her mother would be waiting up for her, which he found totally upsetting, and then he said, "I don't wanna go back; let's just take a walk somewhere," and she said, "OK." He turned up his collar and they walked through Fayetteville, the "coolest small town in America," where many of Southern West Virginia's hipster elite had made their neighborhood. There was a diversity of people out: laughing, talking, riding their bikes, twirling their nose rings, and going about their New Year's Eve seemingly unnoticed and uninterested in noticing what anyone else was doing. It was difficult for Jamie to imagine that not so long ago this was a country allergic to diversity, addicted to racism, and infected with the persecution bug. There were already several other locally owned businesses: two good restaurants, a coffee shop, and a couple of small bodega-like groceries. There was a Vietnamese health place coming, an artisan barbershop, a fish taco cart and Mexican *tienda*, and a Thai place under construction. These mixed with businesses operated by older Fayetteville residents on the street—a nail salon, the bicycle store, and another convenience store—and also a couple of hipster bars and two typically country sports bars. The look was slowly changing, a second bourgeois city was expanding its borders within Southern West Virginia, and Fayetteville was beginning to look like a child's drawing of Portland or Brooklyn. As one bloomed the other one faded, because there wasn't room for both to exist in the same place at the same time, and Jamie couldn't decide if this was a good thing. They came to the "end of the road," and he looked down into the dark holler and thought there was a kind of swirling chaos that seemed to lie deep at the heart of its existence.

"You should come to New York with me," he said. "Could be fun."

"You think I'm better than girls in New York City?"

"You're different."

"They prettier?"

"They ain't as goofy or giggly, I guess."

She frowned.

"Now you know I didn't mean it like that. I like that you're goofy. Girls in New York aren't as funny. Most of them don't have a sense of humor. People always treat this place like some kinda paradise. And it might be at first. Funny thing, though, it's only after everything—living it—that you realize it's nothing."

"Don't you have anyone in New York?"

He thought of Sara, and for a minute that made him uneasy to be around Jen: he felt guilty in some way. "To be totally honest with you, there is someone living with me right now."

She made an audible communication that might've been a reprimand.

"Yeah," he said.

"I wonder where I'd go if I left," she said.

"You could come with me, of course."

"Of course. I used to be happy with how things were going—"

"You could come with me."

"When?"

"Tomorrow morning."

"But you don't know anything about me."

"I know people every place I go think I'm different—New York, West Virginia—they all look at me a certain way and they talk to me a certain way. In a way that you don't."

He was drunk and on the verge of tears about this whole thing.

"Is it really that easy for you to just disappear? What about your family?"

"My life," he said, "is ridiculous. I'm a freak. No, but seriously—my family, I can't even talk to them. I don't love them. How could I? How could anyone love this? I've told myself so many lies about this place I can't remember the truth, let alone admit it. I can't stay here. I can't ever come back here again, and I have no idea what I'm even doing with my life, and I always knew there was something wrong with me, but knowing there's something wrong with you doesn't make it any easier to accept even if you've known it your whole life."

"You came all this way for your dad—that shows some willingness, doesn't it? It shows some..." She looked uneasily down the holler. "It shows some love, right?"

"I just wanna go home, but I don't know where that is."

"Home," she said, "is a place you dream of. It's not a place you ever get to."

They walked back through Fayetteville to their cars, and when they passed the courthouse he looked across the street and saw the professor-looking guy and the aging debutante and for some reason that broke the tension he'd started feeling when Jen said she wouldn't move.

"Hey," he said, "there's that professor-lookin' guy and his wife."

She squinted at them. "Yeah, I think it is, actually."

"Oh my god, we should say somethin' to 'im—"

She said, "No, don't," in this voice like she had suppressed excitement her entire life, and then he was seized with an almost overwhelming desire to prove something and he growled and told her, "Get ready to run," and walked to the edge of the curb and took a deep breath and shouted, *"Hey!"* and the professor-looking guy turned to look at him with his mouth open in surprise and then Jamie said loudly, in his best hillbilly voice, "You're a puppy dog—" and the professor-looking guy said, *"I beg your pardon?"* and Jamie said, *"—real sweet but dumber'n shit!"* and then, *"Run!"* and he and Jen ran away and around the corner and he regretted the pathetic hillbilly imitation in his voice. In his own ears his voice had the quality of a lie. He looked over at Jen, and though he was laughing and satisfied by what he'd done, she was staring at him in a vaguely disapproving manner.

"What?" he said. "What's wrong?"

"Nothing—go, go," she said.

Once they'd reached the cars on the other side of Secret Sandwich, she said, "I thought tonight was really fun. If you're ever in town again, send me a text."

"God," he said, "I hope you're not mad at me over that asshole—"

"What? Oh god, no, I just..." She paused. "I was just scared."

The expression on her face made him realize something and she noticed.

"I swear," she said. "Don't feel bad. It was funny, OK?"

"OK," he said. "It was really great meeting you."

"Yeah, you too," she said. "I'll add you on Facebook, OK?"

"OK," he said, "sounds great. Good night, be careful going back."

She got in her car and drove away, down the road, into the night. He kept thinking of all the reasons he could be standing there, that night, but none came to mind. He thought about what he'd realized earlier: that there was no place for him in this world or in his family.

He wondered why he kept living in a place that wasn't real.

22

IT WAS AN HOUR BEFORE MIDNIGHT and Jamie pulled into the parking lot at Raleigh General and smoked a cigarette and then walked through the automatic doors. The admitting nurse let him in and he rode the elevator up to Janice's floor and then walked down the hallway, and it was a ghost town and everything smelled like a vague mix of cleaning supplies and urine and medicine and latex and rubbing alcohol, and then he got to the room and there was a long pause and he just stood in the doorway, arms at his sides. Carol was there and she was chewing gum and carefully blotting her lipstick, and Janice was in bed and turned toward the TV that was flickering blue with *Dick Clark's New Year's Rockin' Eve*, and the machines churned on, interrupted by the beeps of a series of diagnostic screens that displayed numbers that were meaningless to him. He stepped into the room and said, "Hey," and Janice turned around, ready to smile at whoever just spoke to her, but when she saw it was him she seemed confused and she didn't say anything.

"Thought I'd drop by and see you," he said.

"I thought you left already," she said.

"Oh no, no," he said. "I'm still here. I'm here. Why'd you think that?" He hugged her tightly and she hugged him, and he felt the abrasive fabric of her hospital gown.

"Jamie?" she asked, pulling back. "Are you OK?"

"Yeah, I'm all right," he said. "Why do you ask?"

"You just seem so... sad."

"Just tired, I guess." He reached into his coat pocket and brought out his iPhone and pack of Blacks and absently laid them next to Janice on the bedside table.

"Bad habit," she pointed out.

He pulled up a chair and sat in it backward like a 1990s DARE counselor and then watched *Dick Clark's New Year's Rockin' Eve*, except it wasn't Dick Clark, it was Ryan Seacrest, and he was introducing Pitbull on one of the concert segments.

"Where's Dick Clark?"

"I think he died, didn't he?" Carol said.

"Yep," Janice said, "earlier this year. Was that stroke I thought."

"I knew he had a stroke a few years ago," he said, "but I didn't know he"—clearing his throat, voice cracking apart—"died. We always watched him as kids."

Happier days, naturally. Oh, much happier.

Pitbull was on TV and Janice watched passively. "I don't recognize this person," she said. "Who is this guy? He looks so young."

"What is he, like Mexican or somethin'?" Carol said.

"His name's Pitbull. I think he's Cuban. I don't know his real name."

They sat there watching the concert segment a moment.

"So what'd you do tonight, Jamie?" Janice said.

He said he had dinner with the girl who runs Tamarack, the gallery in Beckley.

"Well, that's fun. Are you excited to go back tomorrow?"

"It's just... back to reality," he said.

Later, Janice wanted a cup of ice, so he and Carol went down the hall to the vending machine closet and filled a cup with ice and Carol asked him something.

"So, New York really changed you?"

"Why do you ask?" he said.

"I'm sorry about earlier. You just seem really different. Did it?"

"I guess it did," he said after a long pause.

"But *how* did it change you?"

"I'm less..." He paused. "I'm less... something. I don't know."

"I want to be changed, too," she whispered like Charles Manson. "I mean, I want to be *changed*. I been thinkin' a lot. I been gettin' this feeling I ought to move away and start my life over. I hate myself so much"—she started crying—"I just sit around the house and do nothin'."

She stared at him like he was holding some secret he could give her. But he had no secrets and he couldn't give her anything. Every day of the past six years—which had, he thought, felt like a century the way time and things change—he worried she wouldn't ever change even though somehow he always thought she would, and the truth was that she had. She stood before him changed, but she couldn't see it.

"Well, a change of place can change who you are," he said.

"When you left did you want to leave forever?"

"You bet I wanted to," he said. "But every time I tried I could feel something pull me back, these invisible arms."

She said nothing, watching him thinking.

"You get to love the place you come from, or your home, or whatever you want to call it," he said. "You get to know every little detail about it. Exactly what it can offer, exactly where you fit in. It becomes an extension of you when you think about things, do things. But at the same time you love it, you hate it. You run it down into the ground, curse it at every turn, tell people it's a bad place. Before long, you're watching it rot from the inside out, watching it get poisoned; you wait too long to escape. Then, when you're thinking about where you fit in, you start to think about what it's taking from you, like it's a vampire or some kind of monster. But still, you always love it. Even though the inside is poison, you love it. Here," he said, handing her the ice cup, and then they started out. "Where would you move to?"

"I know daddy always wanted to go to Tennessee."

"Tennessee sounds so... happy. Tennessee."

Her weak, sad eyes rested on him a moment. "Tennessee."

On *Dick Clark's New Year's Rockin' Eve,* Ryan Seacrest was talking about the events of the past year and then he told someone to "start the countdown" and a timer appeared in the lower third of the screen. People started celebrating and blowing whistles, and they watched the countdown and the ball fall in Times Square as it hit zero, and Ryan Seacrest and Fergie from the Black Eyed Peas were struggling to open a bottle of champagne and confetti was falling and people were kissing and all those same people were happy and it was 2013.

"Happy New Year," Janice said. "2013. Can you believe it?"

"Happy New Year," Jamie said. He felt emotional, so he went to the window and saw the Little Dipper near the horizon and started sobbing quietly, thinking about the time his father, in his own way, had taught him the constellations. When a good memory about him like that one came into Jamie's mind, he used to try to hold on to it and maybe think of other good ones. But after talking to Cortis, he knew now that one good memory didn't necessarily make a good man and that even good men have secrets. And that would never fade or diminish. He wanted to make a comment about his father's death—he needed someone to verify it for him—and when he did his voice was dry. "We never figured out Dad's services."

"You're right, we never did, did we?" Janice said. She took a giant breath and then continued in her tired voice: "Do you still have that goat carving?"

He acted as if he hadn't heard her. He wanted answers, wanted to tear down this wall he'd built up against her, but he wondered if it was worth doing.

"I want to see it again," she said. "I want to."

"Why?" he said, almost afraid. He took the carving from his pocket and felt like he was being dragged through deep water by a chain hooked to a freighter.

She took the paltry carving and studied it, her eyes flat and soul-dead, like a wood carving of herself. "Sometimes I think about the things he wanted to do back then, Jamie, when we was newly married and hungry. He never felt ashamed at all." She slowly shook her head. "But sometimes I did."

"Just tell me," he said.

"He was so young, he wasn't ready to be a father. Oh, Jamie," she said, and started to cry. "He was so, so mean. He wanted to do somethin' wrong."

Jamie stared at her and she was looking at the goat carving real steady, like her world had taken on much larger dimensions than she ever dreamed possible.

"You know who you should talk to?" she said. "You should talk to Juanita. She's stirred up crazy stuff, but she might have somethin' to say."

Jamie's face drained. Juanita was his grandmother by way of his father, and he'd always been told that she was an "evil witch," someone who could go into scary places and come out with real-world powers, powers that could turn a nonbeliever into a believer. There were reasons, lots of them apparently, that he hadn't even thought of her in coming home, hadn't thought of how she would feel about her son's death, nor had she been mentioned by his other family. Even so—even if he hadn't spoken to her since he was five years old—he realized his five-year-old's fear of her remained.

"Is everything OK?" Janice asked.

"No, no—I'm fine. I better get some sleep. Long trip tomorrow."

Janice looked disappointed and said, "Are you sure?" sheepishly, and he said, "Yeah, I... I gotta," paused, and then finished with "get some sleep," and Janice returned the goat carving to him and said, "Well, I love you, son. I was glad we got to see ya. Be careful up there. We'll try to get those services figured out and you can come back down for them if you want to," and he said, "That'd be fine. Love you, too," and he thought he should say good-bye to Carol even though she was awkward and shy, so he said, "Bye, Carol," and she said, "See-ya," sheepishly, and then he got his iPhone and cigarettes and headed out but stopped at the door and turned around to look at them and they both sat there watching TV, and Janice turned to him without looking at him, as if he were a stranger.

"If you go to your Maw-Maw's," she began, "your dad's pistol is in the top drawer of our dresser. Put it on your belt, son."

ABOUT TWO MINUTES SHY of one o'clock, Jamie pulled into Juanita's driveway and parked where the driveway met a cattle gate suspended between two oak posts. He immediately wished he'd brought the pistol his mother offered, but he just didn't believe in it anymore. He doused the headlights and then got out, and his foot had fallen asleep so he climbed, carefully, over the cattle gate and saw two black snakes bundled up, mating—no, *fucking*—on the road and he shivered, thought about turning back, but he was on a mission, as he believed, so he walked a wide circle around them and continued toward the house. The house wasn't much: an old two-room shack with a rough two-by-four porch and chipped white paint, covered in a strange obsidian ash, and a little chimney poking out the top, sitting on the backside of his grandpa's two acres, across a ridge from his parents' house, and on a different driveway from theirs altogether. It was something built by amateur hands, but it was something that would never crumble. As he neared the front porch, a dog of irregular shape snapped at its chain and started barking its throat raw, and Jamie started trembling in a truly wacky manner. He saw silhouettes of a small barn and back porch. He crossed the yard to them and he somehow knew that tonight was *his* night, the night his reckless behavior was just waiting for since he was born, and that he'd end up, most likely, in a shallow grave. He took out his iPhone to turn on the flashlight, and in the black glass the reflection of the moon gave his face the tint of an old-timey picture.

At the back porch, he noted the nail-board (a trap set by hillbillies to stop trespassers) right below the bottom step and was careful to step over it. He skirted a rain barrel and looked inside and saw a mess of shit in there, animal guts and crap that'd be hard for him to forget. He saw baby dolls hanging from fishing-wire nooses, jack-o'-lanterns from Walmart, and a card table, just a little old playing card table, which had a big-ass dead(?) raccoon on it. He stood at the screen door. The shades were drawn and the lights were off, but he swore he could hear a radio playing. He was still hearing the dog barking at its leash when he knocked.

He knocked again and still there was no answer.

He turned the knob. The door wasn't locked. There was a kind of Devil's magic behind it all, he thought, like it was all just a strange and twisted dream. He stood there and thought about a million horror movie scenes, urban legends, old wives' tales, words from his father.

He turned the knob all the way and let himself in.

The inside of the house was a screenshot of a Depression-era Appalachian family. Old woodstove on which a flame danced under a massive pot, cooking a frothy orange substance. A rocking chair sat in the corner, nice enough in its time but since worn out. Washtub hanging from the wall. Curtains reminiscent of a Walmart home-decorating sale or something similar. Jug of moonshine on the floor. Cud of Red Man tobacco, already chewed, stuck to the edge of the porcelain sink, ready to be chewed again. There was a handmade walnut chest that contained firearms of all calibers, many of whose serial numbers had long been filed off. In the bedroom were three sets of bunk beds and one queen-size bed. The walls in the dining area were coated with a faded floral wallpaper and covered with ancestral family photos, from five or six decades, the eyes of which were always watching. Or maybe begging to die.

Jamie looked at the rocking chair and then went quietly toward the bedroom when he heard a pop in the air and smelled the smell of burning hay, a magical farm smell. The smell rose from the floor and lay heavy in the room, and when he turned around, his Maw-Maw, the woman everyone called Juanita, the way he had it told to him, was sitting in the rocking chair.

Forget what year it is, forget what century it is—some things last longer than time. Where the real world meets the woods—that's the only place where magic still exists.

Juanita had appeared in a puff of burning hay. She wore a threadbare T-shirt that read HUG ME, I'M FROM ARKANSAS, bib overalls, and no shoes. She had a Cher haircut, jet-black hair that looked like the wings of something hungry. Judging from her posture, she stood near six-foot-two, a giant, practically, even among men, and probably weighed about 160, horse muscle to the heels, and, honestly, looked like his father wearing a Cher wig. Then there were her eyes, those black, mean, and burning eyes, which were all over Jamie.

"Well, hi, Jamie," she yelled. "That is you, ain't it?"

He thought about tackling her, but he thought too long, then the chance of it was gone.

"I'm gettin' about to be hungry." She paused to look and then asked the most important of all down-home questions: "Stew's about done. You hungry?"

"N-not really, but thank you. I appreciate it."

"You know we're related?"

"Yeah"—he laughed—"I know that."

"Well, that's about the only reason I didn't just now kill you."

He could feel his heart thumping.

"I thought you lived in New York," she said, tending to the stew, maybe sounding afraid, but it was the other way around—he was afraid of her, a cold lump of anxiety back in his throat again. Still, in a few sentences, he tried explaining his life. When he finished, she sighed. "You're just a little feller funnin' around."

The changing expressions on her face were way out there, man, like Charles Manson types of expressions, ones Jamie had seen in many of his family members' faces. "But wild dogs only come outta the woods when they're hungry, Jamie. What're you doin' in my home?"

"I was hopin' you might know somethin' about Dad."

"You want to know everything," she said, pointing at the cupboard in the corner. "There's a bottle of Jack Daniel's in that cupboard. Be good to your Maw-Maw."

Jamie went to the cupboard and found the half-empty bottle of JD among stacks of paper plates and disposable cutlery. He gave it to Juanita, and she unscrewed the cap and then took a sip and wiped her mouth with the back of her hand and passed the bottle back to him.

"Shame about your daddy. Did he jump or what?"

"You don't seem too upset about it. No wonder."

"No wonder what?"

Jamie shrugged. "No wonder I haven't thought of you in so long."

For some reason this seemed to please her.

"You think he maybe fell off?" she ventured.

"Fell off?"

"Off the bridge. Like an accident."

"No," he said, as if he'd explained it all. "It wasn't an accident."

She took this in. "Shame about him. He was a good man. Your mommy said once he was really supportive. Not that I'd ever seen him but twice in twenty years. You remember why he kept you kids from comin' around me?"

"I remember somethin' about turkey feathers."

"Yep, you found a buncha turkey feathers and tied 'em up on the clothesline and your daddy accused me'a stealin' 'em and he said he didn't want me around you kids."

Jamie half laughed. So many things people would never understand about each other, so many things they'd ignore, so many things they'd never know, and there would always be a distance between them that could never be bridged; it was all he could think about.

"Anyway," she continued, "he wanted things to be fixed for us. He tried to have this heart-to-heart talk with me—tell me all about how I caused all his problems, how I cursed him. He told me right in the middle of the night he got hit with somethin'. Some sadness about that damn goat and everything. And once he felt it he knew what he had to do."

"What night? When did he come see you?"

"This was some months back, oh, middle of October, I'd say. Musta been, I don't know, late. Real late. I don't know what time, but it was late, 'cause I was asleep and the TV was all info-commercials. He stood right there where you're standin'. You'd've thought he was a twenty-year-old kid again 'stead a forty-seven-year-old man from the look on his face. I thought, maybe, possibly, he was comin' to atone for what he done."

Some line had been crossed, and Jamie's expression must have blanched, because she asked angrily, "Did you hear what I said? I said maybe he was comin' to atone."

"I'm listening," Jamie said.

"Well, you were sorta distracted."

He didn't want to tell her that he was having nightmares, the one where his dad was dead in the woodpile, for some reason, the worst. "Why?" There was nothing combustible about him now, like somebody had dampened his match. "Why would he do this over a goat?"

"The way your daddy talked, he was like a demon, like Steamboat was this odd sorta demon or somethin', the way he always haunted him."

"Whatever happened to him?"

"Steamboat? Worm-crawlin'." She took a tiny key from a chain around her neck and went to the bedroom and then came out with a mauve-colored box with a giant Native American head painted on it and unlocked the box with the key. She flipped the lid, carefully ran her hands past old photographs, past a few whatnots, to the brown drawstring pouch hidden in the bottom of the box. She looked at Jamie and then took the pouch and gave it to him. "First, let me hear you say it—you reckon you're old enough to hear it?"

"Yes."

"Open the bag."

He slowly untied the drawstring and reached inside, and his hand came out with a deer antler, solid white and preposterously long. One side had been sharpened into a blade and blood had dried in dark red streaks on the knife's edge. Jamie stood there waiting for some enlightenment, as Juanita's eyes stared straight ahead, mind lost in a potent moment.

"For people like your daddy, a family comes along and he thinks he's losin' somethin' of himself. That give him one of his ideas he couldn't keep to himself. The idea he got, because he figured he could sell it and pay for your mommy's operation, see, was that he could steal a goat. When he couldn't do it, he said it was 'cause I cursed him. So I made up somethin' about this antler and he—well, he thought he was sacrificin' it to somethin', some magic. Somethin' I made up. I let him believe that. He had secrets and you'll need to adjust yourself to that. That's how it is. So short. So damn short. Life is about nothin' but answers to you and the many like you."

Jamie just kept nodding, unable to speak for a moment. He turned the bloody antler over in his palm and then wiped his forehead with the back of his hand. "I should head back," he said. "Thanks."

"Back to where?" she asked.

Jamie winced; the question seemed so unbelievably cruel.

"I didn't tell you no lie, Jamie."

"About what?" He was so fucking confused.

"What I mean is you never asked, so I never lied. About the turkey feathers," she said. "I loved the way they looked. All them turkey feathers hung upside down in the summer sun. The way they looked, the way they looked ready to burst into fire. I loved all that."

JAMIE FELT A KIND OF plangent wonder as he drove south along Route 19 back toward Raleigh General and he kept the Jeep at a steady run, blowing by all the generic Appalachian things he'd never wanted for himself. Trailer parks. Coal mines. Convenience stores—Go-Mart, Sheetz, Little General—all that. The mountains were black, two-dimensional apexes against the night sky and he realized he'd miss them when he left forever. He'd miss them in the way he'd miss an arm that'd been cut off. He came to the New River Gorge Bridge and it stretched out before him like an infinitely long ribbon emerging from a magician's sleeve. His father had jumped off that bridge, died of something Jamie understood, something to do with a sadness, "the true thing," and left him with a wish that he were still alive. He drove onto the bridge and then eased the Jeep onto the shoulder and parked, and the bridge, which had seemed to rush alongside him as he drove across it, came to a stop as well and he cut the engine and clutched the door handle.

He got out of the Jeep and found himself at the edge of the bridge some yards away and soon he was looking out at the mountains. He pulled Steamboat the Goat from his pocket and placed it on the railing, and then he climbed the railing and from there he looked down into the gorge a quarter mile deep, nearly a mile across. There'd be nothing to it, he thought, to just step out there. He started to cry and then he thought about his father; in fact he believed he felt his father's ghost or that of something like it in the wind.

He stood there. The wind settled into gusts, not hard but cold.

He was making a decision.

In that moment he closed his eyes and felt as if he were flying from the railing and gliding above the New River, which ran like a pre-Luminist detail through the mountains. He grew smaller in the dark open sky and with every heartbeat his body shook.

He had to catch his balance. And then he stepped from the railing.

And back from the edge of the bridge.

And then he got in the Jeep and put it in gear and drove to the end of the bridge and parked at the vista point, and he stood on the deck with his long shadow hitting the slope below. There was still some part of him that hoped to intersect with his father. He imagined, in the movie of his life, that they'd find each other in the gorge ("after being kept apart for many years") and his father would have a beard and robes and tell him the secrets of the mountains, the soul; tell him so matter-of-factly that it'd suggest he'd known them all along. He was wet and his hair was sizzling with snow and the wind played in and out of his coattails. He had to rescue his father from the underworld. He jumped the deck and headed down into the gorge, and the slope was snow-softened and slick and he had to scrabble at roots and outcroppings to keep from falling, but then suddenly, predictably, he did fall, and for some reason he imagined Steven Tyler's voice just wailing as his body arced and twisted down toward the New River.

The blow to his guts as he smacked the surface of the water knocked the wind out of him and the water rushed up and pulled him under, rinsing his insides, and his limbs were going numb in the freezing water and he was surprised that it was happening so quickly, and then when he couldn't stay afloat he tore off his coat, sinking farther as he wrestled it off. He started making swimming strokes, dumbly, adrenaline washing through him, afraid. Water for blood, blood for water. He heard a cold voice whisper that people have to let things go—fathers and sons, land and blood—and that dying is inevitable.

This was what the cold voice assured him.

This was what it promised.

You want to know how this ends?

JAMIE PADDOCK WAS BORN in West Virginia in 1988 in a single-wide trailer. His parents were Roy and Janice, and Jamie was their first child at eight pounds, two ounces, three testicles.

Roy worked at Angler's Roost, a local sporting goods store in Summersville, and made $3.85/hour. All the usual clichés for describing Appalachian people might've fit him, but none would be fully adequate. He was irascible, of German descent, usually a good deal hardworking but, nevertheless, willing to cheat and steal and fight dirty to survive. He had an old-fashioned face, like someone out of the 1950s: a good-looking man—sharp jaw; short, thick, very dark hair with, in his sideburns, just a few gray strands that were straighter than the rest—and he always wore the same old boots, the rigid hard-toed variety that coal miners wore. While he was still a boy a curse was put on him. His mother put menstrual blood in her pasta sauce to get him "under her power," and he ate the sauce and she said: "You and your son will have no voice; you will never reach fifty and you will die unheard and unloved." This happened in 1969, when Roy was only four years old. What struck one about Roy was his voice: he had this stutter, especially on the vowels, repeating grunts so severe that they became a language of their own.

He never believed this was a result of his mother's curse.

Meanwhile, Jamie's mother, Janice, was a resilient, placid woman: she took care of her siblings (she was slightly older) with no assets, and she was scraping a living working a series of waitressing jobs—Rax, Shoney's, Burger King—when she met Roy. At that moment, she was not a sick woman. She was tough, vital, and, moreover, extraordinarily independent, especially for a woman who grew up in those macho times. She had strong legs that dug solidly into the earth each time she took a step. Her legs were so strong that they could've taken her away from West Virginia, all the way around the world, and then back to West Virginia, one lap around the globe, giant steps just one right after another. She was always in perpetual motion: cleaning, shelving, cooking, going to the store to pick up this, buy that, et cetera. She wasn't a sick woman.

In the space of a year Roy and Janice married and had a child.

And they named the child Jamie.

It wasn't that he was a beautiful baby, nor was he exactly a smart baby. Rich gives birth to rich, poor gives birth to poor, and trash gives birth to trash, and that's how it is, and he was trash, and no one with a lick of sense would've given him a second thought in this great big world. He grew up in the food-stamp hollers of West Virginia and drank off-brand Mountain Dew and had this funny stuttering accent. He had a pair of shoes from Walmart, a pair of cutoff shorts, two pairs of mid-calf socks, and a T-shirt that said ALMOND JOY'S GOT NUTS on the front and MOUNDS DON'T on the back, and that's what he had. And in the summer he spent whole days in the woods with his .22, never bathing, doggedly chasing the fairy diddles like the wild boy he was, and the thought of leaving West Virginia never occurred to him.

He'd go in the woods. He was pure in the woods.

He knew the woods like a scout or some kind of animal. Once he found an arrowhead on the ground near the Indian Rock, just south of their house. He noticed the arrowhead lying under some leaves while mossing with his father. He picked it up and held the talisman in his hand—that's what it was, rather than a rock; a magical talisman almost two inches long, good for a paperweight—and before long he felt it vibrating with the ghosts of Indians.

He'd go in the woods with his father because they realized they'd eat better if they hunted rather than rely on food stamps. So they'd save what food they were given and use it for bait. He was taught to hunt rabbits, squirrels, pheasants, deer—whatever they could kill, cook, and eat. They'd sit with fishing poles at the edge of Cortis's pond and try to catch bass for dinner. They'd peel weeds off their lures and keep threading fresh minnows on to their hooks, and after several hours they'd catch only a few small bass, but they'd take them home in a Walmart bag all the same, and then when they'd get home he'd sit at the picnic table with his father and he'd turn a knife over the flesh of the bass and throw the remains into the woods.

Food was food. Meat was meat. Ah, meat. It was such a rare thing.

This was in the United States of America in the year 1991.

The first time Jamie ever ate at a restaurant was in the summer of '93. He was wearing a red T-shirt with a pair of red cotton shorts and—because he'd just seen the movie *Pale Rider*, starring Clint Eastwood, on an HBO free preview—a pair of little-boy cowboy boots. His parents must've had some extra money because they took him to McDonald's and said he could have anything he wanted, so he said he wanted the McPizza and it took so long to make that they had to pull over in the waiting spot in the parking lot. He waited fifteen minutes—fifteen minutes!—and talked about the McPizza, and then the McDonald's employee brought the McPizza and gave it to Roy through the window, and then Roy gave him the box and he put it on his lap and the box was *so hot* in his little red shorts but he still ate the McPizza until he thought he was going to be sick. This was something *good*. A good place to eat.

McDonald's was something fancy, a once-a-year kind of place.

"You ate that right quick, boy," Roy said. "You get enough?"

Jamie patted his stomach. "That oughta do me till dinner."

Roy laughed and Janice laughed and they drove home.

And in the early fall of 1993, Jamie started school at Mount Lookout Elementary. He'd never seen so many kids in one place in his life, and he watched them with a mixture of fear and wonder. He met a boy named Kenny Bennett who asked him if he'd ever been to Myrtle Beach, and Jamie said, "Is that somewhere past Charleston?" and Kenny started laughing and Jamie suspected at that moment how big the whole damn world was. And because of this the world became threatening to him in a vague way he couldn't work himself out of for a long time.

And he discovered a dark side to life at that unusually early age.

Growing up, he'd often spend Friday nights at Kenny's house. They'd eat pizza from Pizza Hut and rent *The Sword in the Stone* from Kountry Mart and listen to Kenny's mom talk about every incarcerated husband in Southern Regional and play on the PlayStation. Kenny's dad was a coal miner, so Kenny had sixty-dollar Nikes, a satellite dish in his backyard (transmitting the Disney Channel, Nickelodeon, MTV, and Fox on his TV), and a refrigerator full of Mountain Dew. It was absurd, really, how much Kenny had compared with Jamie, but it never would've occurred to Jamie that Kenny's family was any different from his family, or perhaps—more surprising still—any *better* than his family. He was happy with his only T-shirt, the one that said ALMOND JOY'S GOT NUTS on the front and MOUNDS DON'T on the back, and his off-brand Mountain Dew. He was much happier than he remembered being, though I suppose that could just be a memory.

One Friday evening after school, Kenny took the bus to Jamie's trailer for a sleepover, and Kenny said he was hungry and then Janice slapped four slices of bread on the plate that had Jimmy Carter's face on it and put a hot dog in the middle of each, squirted ketchup on them, and rolled them up, and then Kenny looked at them and said he wanted a pizza from Pizza Hut and Janice said, "Well, we don't have any pizza from Pizza Hut, so hot dogs it is," and then Jamie and Kenny took their hot dogs into Jamie's bedroom and Kenny unpacked his backpack and hooked up his PlayStation to the thirteen-inch TV and put in the *Final Fantasy VII* disc.

"Why won't your mom just get us a pizza from Pizza Hut?" Kenny said.

"I dunno, but I thought you liked hot dogs," Jamie said.

"Now they remind me of dicks," Kenny said.

Jamie looked at the Jimmy Carter plate and the hot dogs that looked like penises and the puddle of ketchup oozing out of the bread, and then Kenny played *Final Fantasy VII* and, when he came to the part where you name your hero, he named the hero "Fuckindick."

"Don't name him Fuckindick, Kenny," Jamie said, eating his hot dog.

"Why, 'cause your family's poor and your dad's a hillbilly?"

Against Jamie's better judgment, he punched Kenny in the stomach and Kenny vomited six soft tacos from lunch, and Jamie suddenly realized their entire friendship had only happened because they were two boys who lived in the same town in West Virginia and nothing else.

After taking Kenny home, Jamie wondered if he'd been mean to him. And maybe he had. But Kenny had made him feel like a member of an uncouth herd, and a member of an uncouth herd, it seemed to him, had the right to put a hurtin' on the couth herd—a hurtin' on its people, a hurtin' on what they would and wouldn't do, a hurtin' on who they were and who they weren't.

And it was in the West Virginia of his birth that he remained to grow to plain manhood. He felt at home in the great mountain country, though not quite, as an emptiness clung to the word in a way he couldn't express. He was lonely—I mean, he was so *lonely*—and he'd sometimes late at night plunk himself down in front of the TV and watch anything that was on Cinemax to kill time, or maybe it was to kill the emptiness, and he'd go into his bedroom and jerk off into a pillow until it was crusty and then nothing shocked him anymore, and when you have nothing everything seems acceptable, violence seems normal, and hard-core porn goes by the book, and, after all, porn doesn't actually do any harm, except for when you watch it and then go into your bedroom and you don't even jerk off, you just hold the pillow and cry.

In middle school, someone gave him *On the Road*, asking him to have a look, no mention of who Kerouac was, and he began reading and got to know the great works of all writers and would read and ride his bicycle to the woods and he felt something open, like a space in his head, like his head was a house and he'd been living his entire life in the basement; it opened up rooms in him, back rooms, bedrooms, living rooms, upstairs rooms. With this he began to write, and he won a stupid writing contest and got a trophy that looked like Aladdin's lamp.

With high school the mountains became too much and he couldn't bear to look at them anymore, and then he told Roy he thought he'd have to leave West Virginia someday and Roy said, "If that's what you want to do," and Jamie said, "Yes, that's what I want to do," and he had his heart set on studying at New York University and majoring in dramatic writing at Tisch School of the Arts and that one day he could erase West Virginia from his life because The City would, finally, summon him, and it'd be enough to renounce West Virginia and separate himself from it. That was his desperate plan. And his teachers said he wasn't "cut out" for that school. And his adviser warned him that even with good grades he had only a 1 percent chance of getting into that school. And his parents warned him that they'd never be able to afford that school. And his entire family and community said there was no hope—not even the remotest, most unreal of hopes, the kind of hopes that keeps us alive—that a *hillbilly* could go to that school, because, you see, what people on the outside don't realize is how the sense of possibility, real to their touch, eludes those of us in West Virginia. We can't simply choose to be a doctor or a lawyer. We must become these things. Those on the outside can choose according to their preferences. For us, dreams play a small role at best. It's a matter of survival. So we remain coal miners, laborers. Making a living is a thing entirely divorced from the question of whether we *like* our occupations, to say nothing of finding fulfillment from the earning of our paychecks. These notions are the idle thoughts of James Francos. While they dream, we toil on, staring down the mouth of another coal mine.

Jamie got into NYU and filled out the financial aid forms and forged his parents' names and got scholarships and grants and student loans and he was still $10,000 short, so Roy asked his boss for $10,000 and it took a lot of balls and his boss gave him $10,000 but said he could never take another vacation, and then one day shortly before Jamie left for New York City he started to worry about what the city slickers would think of him, what they'd think of the hillbilly. What would Joyce Carol Oates think of him? Would she call him an animal? Guaranteed she would. Would Jonathan Franzen think he was a barbarian? What would all the metropolitan gods think of the hillbilly? Would they see him as some kind of animal crying out against something he couldn't understand? Would they be surprised he wore shoes? Would they make fun of his funny accent? Would they ask his mother for pizza from Pizza Hut when they knew she could afford only hot dogs on slices of bread?

He sat on the porch with Roy and arching high overhead was Orion.

"Kids're gonna ask me how I grew up—I never even thought about that," Jamie said.

"What're you gonna tell 'em?" Roy said.

"I dunno," Jamie admitted, rubbing the arrowhead. "James Franco goes there."

They were quiet.

"Jamie," Roy began, and then stopped. "You'll find your own way. You got to if you ever wanna figure out who you are. But who you are—no matter what you think, you got nothin' to be ashamed of. You might be poor, but you don't stink. You're just like them—you're just like James Franco. Always remember that. Will you remember that?"

It was the closest they'd ever gotten to discussing not only leaving West Virginia but growing up there, too.

"Yes," Jamie told him.

"Promise me."

"I promise."

And those were the words that let him leave West Virginia: he loved his mother but he couldn't stay; he loved his father but he couldn't stay; he loved his sister but he couldn't stay. So he told them he'd be back soon. Mommy, I love you. Daddy, I love you. Carol, I love you.

You are West Virginia. I am leaving West Virginia.

He packed the arrowhead and got in his '91 Dodge and felt the pain of his departure because he'd had one home only and had never traveled. He pointed the car north and then West Virginia began to lose meaning and the word *home* did, too, and this began his struggle to get away, to become another person. As he drove he enjoyed the unending road, and then the distant spires of New York City welcomed him to a land of dreams and the place had overwhelming beauty and he wanted to keep knowing that more awaited.

But from the moment he arrived, everything in New York City fought to put him in the wrong. He came out of the tunnel and The City hit him like he'd just come out of hyperspace, and then he was nearly sideswiped by a cab and traffic no longer moved so slowly that a hillbilly could easily flow through it. As he drove, he imagined there was an anxiety gauge in his head and that the needle was twitching at max capacity and that cartoon steam was shooting out of his ears. There was just so much. So many people. So many buildings.

Daylight was fading by the time he made it to his Twenty-Sixth Street NYU dorm. He pulled around back to where the loading dock was and parked on the curb and sweat came pouring down his face and chest and he was afraid to open the door. He could hear vague conversations and laughter. He was afraid to leave the car because he didn't know what he'd find on the outside. He was afraid that if he left the car he'd leave his old world forever. Of course he had little choice but to open the door and get out, and that's what he did and his hands were shaking so bad he could barely put his keys in his pocket. He walked up to the loading dock at the back of the Twenty-Sixth Street dorm wearing his ill-fitting boot-cut jeans, denim Chuck Taylors, and bright orange American Eagle polo, and he got caught up in a crowd of all sorts of people, people everywhere, all types of people—African, Irish, Mexican, Pakistani, polyethnic people, Chinese—all kinds. Until then, he'd seen faces like that only on *Lost* and Burger King commercials. In thirty seconds he saw more beautiful people than he'd seen in eighteen years in West Virginia.

You might be poor, but you don't stink, he repeated in his mind.

The gate to the loading dock was ajar and he walked through and up to the RA behind a table, and all the NYU students wearing their expensive clothes were staring at him like he was a sweet, dumb puppy dog, and then the RA said, "Name?" and Jamie was so nervous he stuttered his own name and laughed, humiliated. The RA handed him a packet and said it was his welcome packet ("key and student ID, et cetera"), and Jamie turned the packet over in his trembling hands as if something magical might happen to him. Well, sure enough, he had a sensation of things vibrating around him, of something changing and metamorphosing, as he carried his luggage up to his room. He got off the elevator on the seventh floor and, opening the door to his dorm, saw his roommate, Jack Zhang—a Chinese boy wearing yellow pants, a Yankees ball cap, an American Apparel denim jacket in a flattering size, and chunky headphones—cooking something on the stove. Safe to say it was the first time Jamie'd ever met a Chinese person.

"Hi, Jamie?" Jack said, giving Jamie his hand. "It's very nice to meet you."

Jamie shook his hand and said, "Nice to meet you," and bowed in this oddly formal way, and then they both stood there awkwardly and made some small talk about what they were studying, and Jamie could barely even talk and his fear was like the fear from the time in his childhood when he'd first suspected how big the whole damn world was.

He unpacked his shit and slept hard that first night with no dreams and awoke—where? what time?—to the sound of someone knocking on his door.

Jack's voice: "Jamie? You ready for orientation?"

He followed Jack out into The City and they walked to Madison Square Garden and all the new polyethnic NYU students were there for orientation, and then Michael Ian Black walked onstage and talked about how great NYU was and then Dean Sexton walked onstage and talked about how great NYU was and then there was a Q&A and a boy stood up and asked, "What about people who can't afford NYU?" and Dean Sexton must've thought the boy was joking because he said, "If you can't afford it, do you think you really belong here?" like a fucking comedian, but then he must've known from the set of the boy's jaw and his furrowed brow that he was serious because he said, "There are people who can advise you on those situations," and the boy just sat back down and looked at his folded hands in his lap and there was something in his eyes, some pain, that hadn't been there before, and Jamie tried to think of something to say—a question, something—but nothing came to him and he sat there.

Afterward, they walked outside and Jack talked about his plans, and Jamie said he just wanted to go back to the dorm but that he didn't know how to get there, and Jack said, "Just take the train," and Jamie, having never been on "the train" before, started breathing in hard and exhaling, saying, "I can't, can't . . . can't do it. Not even for a little ways... Please—" and then Jack gave him his first Xanax and directions on a piece of paper and said, "You can do it."

Though Jamie, in tears, begged him to stay, Jack left in a cab.

A few blocks from Madison Square Garden, Jamie ended up freaking out real bad and then he walked around the city for three hours. He was just walking around not knowing where he was and he was hungry, and at one point he got his boot-cut jeans caught in a manhole cover and had an anxiety attack right there on the street, until this big black guy set him free and then asked him for six dollars and Jamie gave him all the change he had left. Needing to be bolder than he felt, he summoned up the nerve and took the Xanax and, finding himself going east, crossed Second Avenue to NYU Langone, and he came to an area within whose fenced-in confines were the works of public service and large piles of piping. At the far corner of the area, behind a bulldozer, somebody was working concrete with a jackhammer. There was a solitary trailer and the front door of it was open, and Jamie went inside and he'd never felt so invisible in his life, and a homeless-looking guy was sitting on a couch and the homeless-looking guy straightened up and spoke through his tears. *"This dream,"* he said. *"I'm scared."*

For a year after that Jamie hated New York City. He'd spend days alone in his dorm with nothing to do but rub the arrowhead and let his head trouble him with thoughts of West Virginia and the woods and his family. The few occasions he did go out he would just do what needed to be done, then hurry back, lock the door, breathe in and out deeply, and that was when he knew he was hopeless. But part of him thought: *What is my problem? Why am I struggling?* He'd come to a different kind of world from the one he'd always known, and he realized such a world would require a different kind of person. Over the next several years, he saw the depths of his fear. He cried out against the rich at Zuccotti Park; he shouted his love to the poor. He went to the preacher man at St. Patrick's. He dropped out of New York University. He dove deep into the women he loved. He slept on a bloody twin mattress that belonged to a male prostitute. All for The City. When he took off the orange American Eagle polo and put on the gray sweater, he recognized himself. When he put on a black overcoat and slim jeans and combed his hair up so high that he was three inches taller, he recognized himself. He still drank Mountain Dew as if that were something his breeding wouldn't allow him to give up; it was, perhaps, the only characteristic he'd held on to, but when he sold his car for five hundred dollars and ate that New York pizza and put on Ray-Bans and fucked a city girl, when he changed his accent to obscure the fact that he was from West Virginia, when the city soaked into him and shaped him into the man he was becoming, he recognized himself as a New Yorker and he was happy.

And West Virginia was gone. A dream you just remember.

A vivid memory of something strange and beautiful.

But there was one thing he hadn't forgotten.

You might be poor, but you don't stink.

THE NEW RIVER HEAVED and splashed and then Jamie's head emerged from the water and an instant later, downriver, he found a shallow spot. At some places the bottom got deep and he had to dog paddle, but eventually he was able to ford a few feet of inlet and drag himself onto the sandbar, feeling heavy, his jeans (and teeth) full of what felt like compost. He found his coat, which he then tried to wring out, but the prolonged exposure had tightened his muscles and he began to shudder. He sat at the water's edge for a moment.

The water reflected moonlight onto the sandbar and everything was gray except for the vortices of strong-flowing water, which were night black.

He was dead and his life here was all a dream.

He looked up and saw a tangle of tree branches forming a living cathedral. And, between the leaves and limbs, there was—maybe by strange coincidence, or maybe it was the universe's foreshadowing, he'd never know—a great view of Orion the Hunter.

Jamie thought about the words his father had told him.

You might be poor, but you don't stink.

He said the words to himself until he forgot them.

And when he forgot them, the place—it was gone, too.
In his heart, in his mind, forever.
Like it never existed at all.

JAMIE ARRIVED back in New York around ten o'clock the following night. He came out of Penn Station and it was dark but a little warmer than it had been, and the superbright lights hit him and he heard the modern music (might've been Maroon 5) and then turned east down Thirty-Third Street and walked among the ever-changing mix of people: the Indians, Pakistanis, Africans, Chinese, Japanese; the whites, the blacks, the polyethnic people. He got on the N at Herald Square and rode it down to Eighth Street–NYU, and it was so improbable, all those different people together in one spot, that he thought people who don't think New York City is the most beautiful place in the world are the saddest people in this world.

As soon as he got back he unpacked, and the whole apartment smelled eggily of gas, and he was sore from falling in the river and he took a long hot shower and then noticed his roommate was still gone so he texted her, "You still in Texas? Leaving rent on your desk," and then, when he didn't get a reply, "Back now—see you soon." He wrote a check for $1,000 and left it on his roommate's desk, and then he went through the window onto the fire escape and looked out across an epic view of the city that reached from the historic buildings of the Lower East

Side to the skyscrapers downtown, the dark forests of SoHo to the towers of FiDi, all the way to the Freedom Tower and the southern tip of the island and the edge of the East River.

He smiled faintly and sincerely and then turned and went back inside.

He checked his bank account on his iPhone and saw he had only eighteen dollars and was suddenly aware of how hungry he was and how it was only Tuesday night and he wouldn't have any money to eat until that Friday. He stole some change from his roommate's room and went downstairs to buy a slice of pizza, which he ate on the corner, barely tasting it, before returning upstairs. He could still smell the rotten egg tang of gas and it was so strong that he nearly gagged. He called his building's super, an eastern European named Maarten, and told him, haltingly explaining about the rotten egg smell, and after he was finished, Maarten was quiet.

"Oh, Jamie," Maarten said, sighing, but he didn't sound angry. "If it's as bad as you think it is," and for some reason he laughed a little.

"What should I do?" he asked, and Maarten moaned.

About fifteen minutes later Maarten came up to his apartment and dramatically sniffed the air with his huge nostrils. He kept saying, "It's fine, it's fine," and running his fingers over the dishes in the sink. Jamie tried to tell him again that there was a gas leak, but every time he tried, Maarten made a noncommittal grunting noise. "You ever do your dishes, man?"

He was perplexed and disbelieving. "What do you mean?"

"Your place stink, man," Maarten said. "It's the dishes. They smell."

The idea was so preposterous that it took him a while to understand what Maarten was saying. When he did, he stopped and laughed, embarrassed. "You gotta be kidding, Maarten," he said. "It's not the dishes. This building could blow up, man."

Maarten laughed back at him. "The building's not going to blow up."

Jamie shook his head again.

"You stink," Maarten persisted. "Your neighbor used to ask me about gas as well. And I'd tell him the same thing I told you: do your dishes."

He didn't, couldn't, say anything in response, and Maarten left and Jamie was conscious of his eyelids twitching the way they did when he was exhausted. He called Sara, but there was no answer and he waited and waited and Sara didn't call.

The next morning, he called and called and Sara's phone rang and rang. It was beginning to worry him. He did some laundry and then, later, walking over to Third Avenue in the snow, went into Dunkin' Donuts, where he called a drug dealer named Spyro and asked if there was any possible way he could get some Xanax and Vicodin and pay him Friday, and Spyro, the drug dealer, asked why he hadn't seen him in six months ("I don't know, Spyro, you're so far, it's like two hours away," Jamie said). He walked over to Park Avenue, thinking about Sara, wondering what she was doing, in a state of knowing but also not knowing re: why she hadn't answered his calls, and got on the 6 at Twenty-Eighth Street. At Spring Street he disembarked and walked the six or seven blocks to the former event space where he and Sara had gone to the pharm party. He punched the buzzer for the third floor and then a blond guy with Wayfarers came down and answered the door.

"I'm lookin' for Sara. She here somewhere?" Jamie said.

"I really can't understand it," Wayfarer Boy was saying as they ran upstairs. "I really can't understand it. I really can't understand it at all..."

Through the doors of the third floor, it was nothing like it was the night of the party: the floor was water—not water but sewage or something from a broken pipe; squatters slept on futons among piles of trash and black metal drums full of fire; cockroaches and rats; the rank smell of BO and bad pomade. Jamie wondered, *Where am I? This place, this land of the dead. So many people come to New York, so many people, so many things, every day a million different people come, every day with different things...*

For a minute he saw nothing, just that weird place, and then there, in a pile of bedding, slept Sara, her face buried in a bloody mattress. He crouched down. He said, "Oh my god, Sara," and Sara turned her head from the mattress and looked up at him; her face was goofy in a drugged way and her lips were chapped and parted, showing yellow unbrushed teeth. Her bandage-wrapped wrists, soaked with new and old blood, lay uselessly at her sides. She had a hospital wristband but didn't seem to acknowledge it.

"Put your arm around my neck," he said, and she did and he lifted her.

That night, after he took her to the hospital connected with NYU and admitted her—she'd been docile and narcotized in the waiting room but then had come to and become angry and confused, moaning and turning around, screaming out, jostling, pushing and shoving, clawing weakly against the orderlies as they dragged her down the long corridors, past the consulting rooms and the operating theaters, the surgeries and the wards—he walked outside to smoke and a calendar notification popped up on his iPhone: "Reading at Mellow Pages, Tomorrow, 7:00 PM." He searched Gmail for a .doc of his story and then felt his hands begin to shake; there was something anxiety-inducing about being in a room where he'd have to speak, where everyone was there to be amused by his accent—in a "good-natured" way—and nothing could be done about it.

He went upstairs and, beside Sara's bed, her eyes closed, her hand in his, he practiced reading the story. He read the story over and over. He whispered, "You like it, Sara?"

Her mouth opened and then closed and her fingers tightened and then loosened.

She was dreaming, dreaming bad dreams.

There were nurses and there were doctors and they were giving Sara drugs and giving her medicines, and among the doctors was Dr. Wolfe, a doctor in his forties with an unsettling Manson-like smile. "She has a slight infection," he said. "She eating regularly, sleeping?"

"I really don't know. What kind of infection?" Jamie said.

And in these strange, half-formed moments, Jamie started telling Dr. Wolfe everything: how Sara probably was depressed and how she had a history and how he met her at the fashion design student's party and how she stole his arrowhead and jacket but gave them back.

Finally, as he was leaving, Dr. Wolfe said, "I'm going to recommend this woman be admitted to the mental health wing," and then, "You're shaking."

They went downstairs to the food-to-go counter for food and Jamie looked at the menu. He could've gotten half a club sandwich and a thing of green juice for about twelve dollars but decided on a whole sandwich and a cup of coffee for sixteen dollars so he could have half the next day. He thought about the eighteen dollars in his bank account and worked the math and, spacing out the leftovers from this meal, figured he'd survive through Friday. Dr. Wolfe picked up a falafel and then they went to the counter and Dr. Wolfe paid for everything and Jamie thanked him and said, "Oh, wow, you didn't have to do that," and Dr. Wolfe smiled. They found two chairs and sat and ate their sandwiches and talked: about Sara, who, given her history of self-injury, had to be observed for several days; about Dr. Wolfe, who sometimes lived in a palace in "Westchester" and hated the county; about his son, Little Joe, being born on a kitchen table in Brooklyn; about Jamie's work, where he was from.

"I'm originally from West Virginia," he finally admitted.

"Virginia? You must have really come a long way."

"Yeah, I've changed," he said. "I'm a different person now."

"Where do you live?"

"Second Avenue, between Seventh and St. Mark's."

This registered on Dr. Wolfe's face as he lifted his coffee cup and then, without sipping any coffee, held it aloft and said, "Wow."

"No, really," he said.

Dr. Wolfe smiled in this sarcastic way, but the moment he noticed Jamie staring at him his face became a mask. "Well, that's a very nice neighborhood, isn't it?" He'd said it in such a way that it was impossible for Jamie to tell if he still thought he was lying or if he thought the neighborhood was too nice for someone like him, an ill-bred lout evolving in reverse.

"Yeah," Jamie said. "It's very nice."

In the darkness of Sara's room, he leaned back in a chair and contemplated his arrowhead. It looked dirty.

"What the fuck happened to your hair? It's white."

He turned around, startled, and saw Sara and what can only be described as a rebellious/1990s indie rock expression across her features. He said, *"What?"* and she said, "Your hair— it's white," her throat dry, and then he took out his iPhone and turned on the front-facing camera to check his hair and it was still brown.

"Just kidding. You're so fucking stupid," she said.

"Hey," he said, and then, for being so stupid, "Fuck you."

"It's cold," she said.

"Want me to turn the heat up?"

"I really don't give a fuck," she said indifferently.

He went and cranked up the heat a jag and then sat back down and looked at her, and she was looking back at him in the teasing way he'd become accustomed to.

"Thought I'd never see you again," she said.

"Well, here I am, in my corporeal form," he said half scornfully, but then, more gently, "Sara, you didn't do this because of me, did you?"

"Well, yeah," she admitted. "Look." She lifted her gown and showed him where she'd cut herself. Below her hip, she'd carved a picture of what she said was an arrowhead. She said it was magical and for him. And when he asked her why she'd done it she said there was something sad and beautiful about having a scar, something sexy.

"Goddamn it, Sara," he said. "Why?"

"I don't know," she said. "I don't know. Isn't it beautiful, though—"

"Sara"—and he heard how confrontational he was being as soon as he said it—"I guess I just want to understand why you started doing it—"

"Why don't we start with this: I just figured as long as I had a lot of problems and, um, see, I already can't remember—"

"Oh god, forget it."

"It just made me feel... I don't know, OK? 'Cause all day I'd be thinking like if I make little cuts on each arm evenly, you know, like no one's—who's gonna suspect?"

"No one will ever know..."

"Yeah, so I get home from school and start making little cuts and... I mean, my parents know—they know—everyone knows. I'm like cutting scars on the backs of my hands and everyone knows and no one even cares enough to do anything about it."

"So you just cut yourself too much this time."

"My dad." She sounded tired. "He's an asshole dad, but he has cancer. Found out he was terminal. He's just rotting. And the worst part is I don't even care. I just wish he'd die."

It was an unusual thing to hear and Jamie was rattled by it.

"I am so sorry, Sara."

"No, I'm sorry; it's totally crazy. It's just that I'm not—I'm not a good person. And it only makes it worse to pretend I am. I just think I love you."

This clarified something for him and was part of her appeal: that she was some externalized version of his soul. A distinctly self-centered thing to think, but even so. He was beginning to think that his vanity had become so intense that he'd in fact like to cut himself.

"Jamie, please don't let them keep me here," she said in a low, whispery voice.

"I mean, I guess that'll be up to the doctor, right?" he said.

"Just promise me! *Promise me* you won't leave me here."

"I want you to stay here tonight and we'll see about leaving tomorrow."

IT WAS TEN IN THE MORNING and Jamie was back at the office, going through the refrigerator looking for something to eat, when Amy, the office manager, told him that they'd be having a meeting when Jon, their boss, who was less and less present, arrived, twenty minutes maybe. She left and he leaned against the brick wall and ate a bowl of grapes and then stared out the tenth-floor window that looked over Seventh Avenue. He was sweating for some reason and dreading the rest of the day, and when he turned around he saw Laura sipping a Starbucks coffee.

"Thought I'd never see you again," she said.

"People keep saying that to me," he said, grinning.

She paused. "So, how are you doing?"

He thought about it and wondered if he wanted to tread on that ground. "Oh, I don't know... it seemed... I don't know the word. Awkward maybe or—"

"Difficult."

That was the word that stopped the banter and he thought, *Yes, the past week has been difficult.* "Yeah... I was... God, I didn't recognize anybody..." He realized he was staring at her imploringly in the way that only he could and then he laughed self-consciously.

"Well, you look better," she said, and he heard the relief in her voice.

After a brief pause he admitted, "I feel better."

"That's good," she said, and then, out of the blue: "Did you hear about the meeting?"

"Is it bad? You looked vaguely concerned when you said that."

"Yeah, we don't even know because we still have clients—"

"Nobody can do anything yet, right? Except Jon, right?"

"Right, but maybe it doesn't matter, you know?"

"World's full of surprises. Whatever." After an awkward silence, he pointed out, "Anywa-a-ay, I'm doing a reading tonight. You could, um, come—hey, don't laugh—but whatever."

"I don't know how good an idea that really is," she said somewhat dubiously.

"Oh hell," he moaned, "might take your mind off all this bullshit."

She pondered it. "OK, why not? Where is it?"

He took off his coat and walked through several doors until he reached the open-plan office. It was still the holidays, so much of the staff was on vacation, but he spotted Nadi and Amy behind one of the partitions and Nadi had her feet up on the desk and they were watching a video on a large Mac computer monitor. He popped his head around the partition when he heard his own voice speaking the manga voice-over. In the cosplay-heavy video, the characters acted out a live-action role-playing battle and said a few conventional phrases in Japanese, and then at the end he heard his voice again, that Appalachian twang, and Nadi cracked a joke in an exaggerated hillbilly accent that struck him as repugnant because, though he'd convinced himself he'd shed West Virginia, his instinctive reaction was to defend it. He cleared his throat and Amy and Nadi turned around and blushed. "You make fun of a man behind his back and he hears about it," he said in his default voice, "he's likely to say some things he don't mean."

Twenty minutes later Jon arrived, and they all waited at the long glass table that stood in the center of the main room and no one spoke, and Jamie was generally fuming/semibothered, studying Jon suspiciously for some kind of hint, and then he concluded from the way Jon hunched so low over the table that they were all in fact about to be fired. Jon said, "Please, everyone, have a seat," and they all sat down and he said, "As you know, Monster Media has been reorganizing to refocus our clients and we're faced with significant profit declines and changes in the market. Over the last few weeks I've had to make some very difficult decisions regarding our company and I must unfortunately inform you that we will be closing down operations at the end of the week." Jon passed out the pink slips and said, "I know this is difficult news," and no one said anything for a long time. Chairs were moved, throats were cleared, noses sniffed: extraneous sounds caused by humiliation and awkwardness.

"Is this for real?" Jamie asked.

"It's for real. HR will have resources available to you after this."

"What about About.com??" Amy said with two question marks.

"I talked to About.com on the phone and they blew up. I'm telling you: they hate what they don't understand. They finally have a chance to make some money and they're not interested. They're punishing Monster Media for being forward-thinking. The good news is I'm going to start another company, restructure a bit; that way the nine of us can work together again. But I've got to regain my appetite for advertising, so I'll be taking some time off."

"But figure six months for the investments then—what?—a year to build, another six months to get off the ground? That's a long time without a paycheck, Jon," Jamie said. He had this ridiculous impulse to take off his shoes and dance on the table like someone from *Hee Haw* or something. "So I guess that's it," he said. "Better call your trust officer, Nadi."

Nadi stared at him, uncomprehending, her mouth open slightly.

Amy's head dropped forward and she looked at her feet.

Laura looked confused. "What the fuck, Jamie?"

"Jamie, I know you're angry but have some compassion—"

"Fuck no. These fuckin' people'll make fun of you to your face, Jon. I think you're a great guy—don't ask me why—but I'd rather kill myself than work with them again."

Everyone looked down at their feet and he wiped a hand across his forehead and pulled himself together and walked out. He immediately regretted what he'd said but he just kept walking, and then he glanced back and saw Laura staring at her feet, unable to look up.

He left and started up Seventh Avenue, first veering onto Broadway so he wouldn't have to go into Times Square, and then boarded the 1 at the Times Square–Forty-Second Street station and rode it down to Canal Street, where he disembarked and walked the few blocks to the unemployment office. He went inside and stood in the queue of desperate, tired-looking strangers, those desperate, defeated strangers with their desperate, hungry faces. *This is my world,* he thought, and he thought about all the things he'd learned by coming to New York but couldn't remember how he'd learned them. True enough, he'd escaped a poor childhood spent cutting meat from half-rotten carcasses, having nothing to eat but baked potatoes, and being conservative beyond salvation, but he didn't know how that'd happened. He understood, though, primally, how he'd disappeared into that crowd of desperate, hungry people and that was enough. That was enough.

At noon, Spyro texted him "meet you in a couple hours," so he went back to his apartment and watched *Forensic Files*. At 2:37 he heard the buzzer buzzing far beneath him, announcing Spyro's arrival, and then Spyro came upstairs and gave him a Jiffy bag of pills and he said, "Hey, I appreciate this," and promised Spyro $200 in the future, and then Spyro asked him if he wanted to smoke. Weed made him super paranoid and uncomfortable, but he smoked a couple bowls anyway and then there was this interlude of watching *Forensic Files*—he was too high to really listen, just awake enough to distinguish the strange dialogue: *"My faith in God that he's watching over her and protecting her and that he's going to bring her home to us"... "I really believe that she's still alive"... "The way she was frozen in everyone's memories"... "Christmas... that was Christmas. Thought for sure she was coming home for Christmas. That's when I realized that she was never coming home."*

The narrator was saying, *"A man hiking through the desert outside of Tucson found a skull, which looked like that of a human child."*

Spyro pointed at the TV and said, "Oh shit."

Jamie looked at the TV and saw a human skull, a child's skull, stripped of its skin and lying in the desert, with Hi-C-colored rubies for eyes, and he couldn't look away, for the skull stared back at him. He smiled and said, "Death or some such thing is upon us now."

"Oh fuck," Spyro said. "Didn't know you was so wise. Namaste."

And the TV kept showing that skull. That child's skull.

At the end the mother of the murdered child said something.

She said, *"One time when I was going through a tough time, trying to come to a peace about her death, she came to my bedroom. And I was like— I'm sleeping, and I hear these little pitter-patter of feet—and you have to understand this is after Vicki has been deceased—and here's Vicki standing at the foot of my bed saying, 'Mommy, I'm OK. I need you to be OK.'"*

Spyro left and Jamie swallowed a Xanax and then took the Jiffy bag to the medicine cabinet. He looked at it sitting there on the shelf and then pushed it back a little ways, thinking to put it out of view, and then looked at it for a minute longer before closing the cabinet.

Later he slept on the futon and had a dream within a dream of crawling on his hands and knees through a circle of ash that turned into nightmares of bodies lying everywhere, their eyes still open, their mouths pouring with blood, and then there was a strange calmness. When he woke he looked at his iPhone and saw that it was a quarter to five and at that precise moment he got a Facebook friend request from Jen. He accepted her friend request and then touched her avatar and started typing in chat: "Are you... are you for real?"

"What do you mean?" she typed. "Real?"

29

JAMIE DRESSED QUICKLY and took the L out to Brooklyn for the reading. The train was repeatedly delayed by crowds and then about an hour later he got off at Morgan Avenue and walked around the corner through the snow and mud, waiting to let a hipster-looking guy cycle past him, to Mellow Pages, which was in the artist lofts on Bogart Street near these vacant lots with big bright green trees and sheaves of weeds that smelled good. He stood in the doorway and his stomach tightened and the cramps were so intense that he clutched his waist and sort of doubled over in pain, and then he turned into a vacant lot that was used for art installations. He bit off half a Xanax and then the pain faded long enough for him to stand up straight and go inside. The door to the studio opened to a densely packed crowd of about forty or fifty, writers mostly, all with some sense of discomfort or awkwardness, and only a few of the faces were fixated on him. Someone who looked like Zosia Mamet—mousy brown hair, nonprescription hipster-framed glasses, American Apparel button-down—approached him and leaned in close.

"I thought, *That must be him,*" she said, kissing him on each cheek.

"Hey, here I am," he added lamely. "I'm Jamie—"

She said she was Victoria, the editor of the magazine, and that she "loved the story" and that they were about to get started and if it mattered to him when he read. He said, "I'll go last if that's cool," and she said, "Sounds great. So you came all the way up here from Virginia?" and he felt the animal inside him perk up, aware of danger but unable to escape it, saying, "No, no, no, I live up here—in Manhattan—but I'm from there, well, it's *West* Virginia, actually." He joked that New York was so passé that he might rather be in West Virginia, and then she laughed, encouraging him to laugh with her by touching his chest, which he allowed.

"Oh, well, we just *loved* the story," she gushed.

The other writers were reading their stories, and he was tapping his fingers very loudly on a bookshelf and his eyes were half closed and he was breathing deeply. Victoria introduced him as "a writer from West Virginia," and he went to the front of the room and then opened a copy of the magazine and flipped to his story, and for a moment he thought he was going to cry; he was sweating and he couldn't swallow. He tried to keep his eyes on the page, on his story, but at every cough or shuffle he glanced up and saw everyone staring at him. He began to read his story, carefully measuring each word to sound like that generic Midwest-type accent, and, about halfway through, his voice started to sound hypocritical in his own ears. The audience's judgmental faces—though he figured he might've been overreacting; they probably didn't care—scared him enough to not continue for a beat. Then he let the default voice come back, the hillbilly voice he'd been trying to change for years.

"'I felt like one minute I was in West Virginia, and it was a dream,'" he read, "'and I was happy'"—his voice trembled with emotion—"'and then—and then, well, I realized all the strange, sad, and terrible things that happened to me weren't perfectly normal—but come to West Virginia. Come to the mountains if you want to reveal everything or nearly everything. If you want to listen and be surprised by what you hear, if you want to find something worth finding in the end—come to West Virginia. I thought about it and it didn't seem like such a lie.'" When he paused, he looked at the audience, oblivious to his hypocrisy, which moved him to keep reading: "'Actually, that's a lie right there. There're things you'd never know about West Virginia unless you've lived there. It's ugly. Real mean and real ugly. So ugly in fact that once you've looked as I've looked, once you've stared as I've stared into those eyes, then you cannot look away, for it stares back at you, and it'll turn you into something else, a kind of monster.'"

The editor, Victoria, and even all the writers—they all stared at him as if he'd shattered something precious, or destroyed a mascot that'd been highly regarded.

Later, he was drinking a PBR and standing in the corner, and Chris—a Brooklyn-based writer wearing clear plastic frames and smoking a joint—was comparing his writing style to Pearl S. Buck and Jamie was just nodding to himself, muttering, "Oh yeah, oh fuck yeah." Someone excitedly shouted, "Jamie," and he turned around and saw Laura and she made her way over to him. He looked at her as if stunned and then, blushing, said, "Hey."

"Look—goose bumps," she said, holding out her arm.

"I'm so bad at this," he said, and they sort of stood there awkwardly.

"Oh yeah, what was that about?" she asked. "What happened earlier?"

He closed his eyes, shook his head. "Look," he said. "Earlier. I didn't mean for you to hear all that. I've been under a lot of stress and with Monster and whatever."

"I don't understand. Did something happen?"

"Here's where—here's the thing. It's irrelevant, OK?"

"Shit, Jamie, just tell me," she said.

"You really wanna know?"

"Not really, but yes."

He looked around at all the hipsters. "Let's get the fuck outta here first."

They walked down Bogart a few blocks to this bar called Bizarre and they each had a few beers, and he told her about Amy and Nadi making fun of him and then he told her this story about the poet J. J. Phillips taking the train out to meet great American country blues singer Lightnin' Hopkins and slathering herself with self-tanner because she feared that Lightnin' would reject her because she was too light-skinned and how that depressed him so completely.

"How many times do I have to tell you that this city is filled with horrible human beings?" she said. "Get. Used. To. It. Go to a library. Take a walk in the park."

"You actually believe that?" he said. "Do you really believe that?"

"My opinion is: I guess you shouldn't expect too much from people."

He frowned. "You have a beautiful voice, you know that?"

They left Bizarre a couple hours later and it was dark and snowing so diabolically hard that he couldn't see five inches in front of himself, and then they were walking around the corner to the Myrtle Avenue station and he kept getting that feeling of being followed, but whenever he looked back it was only hipster guys carrying a baby cheetah. The guys—two of them—had dreadlocks and basically looked the same in the snow.

"I keep gettin' that feeling I'm bein' followed," he said.

She looked back. "You don't think it's that serial killer, do you?"

"Oh shit, they never caught that guy?" He just stared for a couple seconds. "We should probably walk faster." He managed a sly grin, which she, of course, noticed.

"That deadpan is impressive," she said, smiling.

They arrived at the Myrtle Avenue station and there was a considerable pause during which the snow fell sideways and cars traversed the snow-covered street.

"I'll see you sometime." She lingered. "Until then, um, I guess..."

"I don't think"—he checked his iPhone—"it's a good idea."

She smiled and stared hard into his face. "And you're totally, totally right. Listen, I wasn't—all I meant to say was I had fun."

"Yeah," he said. "It was a lot of fun. Good night, OK?"

She started moving up the steps to the train, running her hand along the railing, moving away from him, and then he adjusted his collar.

30

JAMIE TOOK THE J BACK to Canal Street, and it was so cold walking up Lafayette to the 6 that his breath came out in jets. He was drunk and his feet moved slowly along the sidewalk through large banks of snow so deep he wished he had a dog sled, and he could smell food cooking in Chinatown and hear the muted, haunting strains of Imogen Heap's "Hide and Seek," and there were half-seen, half-heard figures everywhere in the snow. He descended into the 6 station and waited for a train, and down the platform a woman, baby in her arms, lice in her hair, looked at him and mouthed, "I have places I need to be," and he understood exactly the extraordinary helplessness and desperation she felt.

At the hospital he walked up to the admitting nurse's desk but no one was there, just this sort of semiparanoid feeling that he was unable to shake, and then someone, a janitor, passed by and said something unintelligible. He got on the elevator and rode it up to Sara's floor.

He stood in the doorway of Sara's room and she was standing at the window looking out at the city, unhappy in that twilight zone, but after noticing him she smiled.

"What'd the doctor say?" he said, walking into the room.

"He wanted to cut me open, have a look, see what makes me tick. They wanted to 'move me to a nicer place' where I could 'undergo treatment.'"

"And you think that's like ridiculous?"

"Like I said—none of this is gonna make me a different person."

He thought about it for a long time. He didn't know how he could say no to her even if he still hated her. She was probably right. And even if she wasn't, so what? They'd fucked up both of their lives. They'd both nearly committed suicide, both of them.

"OK, then," he said. "Fuck it. Let's go."

"Are you being serious right now?"

"I'm really, really worried about you. You can stay with me—because you need a place to stay—even though you never told me why *you* smeared *hummus* on *my* wall."

She smiled a thin smile. "And that's why we don't do drugs." She looked at the ceiling and then back at him. "Thank you. I know it's like not easy, y'know?"

He relaxed a little. "You're welcome."

"Did you see any guards on your way up?"

"You don't have the fuckin' plague—"

"No," she said, "no, but I am the Devil, remember?" She made a face and gestured to the two dome-like calcifications on her head. "And if you set me free..."

"Well, if there are guards, I can turn invisible now, so we're good."

"How'd you learn to do that?" she whispered mock seriously.

"And I don't want the world to see *meeeeee*," he sang, pretending to slip a ring on his finger à la *Lord of the Rings*. "'Cause I don't think that they'd under*staaaaaand*. When everything's made to be *brokeeen*! I just want you to know who I *aaaaaam*."

He made a popping sound with his tongue.

"Oh shit, where'd you go?"

He walked out of the room, looking over his shoulder as he made his way through the main hall to the elevator, and then a nurse emerged from a room wearing bloody scrubs and just stared at him like he didn't exist. There was no reaction on the nurse's impassive face, nothing, and then he wiped his hand over his face and the nurse wasn't there anymore. He got to the elevator and punched the down button and started making gestures that didn't mean anything to Sara. She emerged from the room and dumbly walked toward him, dramatically back-lit by the fluorescents, and then they got on the elevator and went down to the main floor. Sara was saying, "Oh shit, oh shit, oh shit, oh shit, oh shit, oh shit," and he was laughing, saying, "Did you see how I was invisible? Did you see how I made the nurse disappear?"

After escaping the hospital, they walked down a very quiet stretch of First Avenue and a light snow was falling and Sara was wearing just her boots and the hospital gown and he imagined this to be the poster in the movie of his life. He took off his coat and put it over her shoulders, and he tried to but couldn't fathom what she wanted for herself in life. Now bundled in his coat, she marched ahead and he followed in a sweater, sobering up, quietly shivering.

She asked him if he found out anything about his father.

"Yeah." He laughed a little too loudly. "He was really into these wood carvings and all this stuff and... oh shit, whatever. I know he's gone and everything, but..."

"But what?"

"But it's crazy how you never know about people. Like what's the point?"

"The point is you don't know," she added.

He smiled vaguely. "You know, I used to be the biggest redneck in the world. Like I cried when Dale Earnhardt died—"

"Are you serious? You're all over the place—"

"Yeah, I was like twelve, but I cried. I always wanted to be a different guy, though. Like when I was in third grade there was this new girl in school and she said, 'Have you heard about this new band, the Goo Goo Dolls?' and I said no and then she said, 'Their lead singer is *sexy*,' and when she said that I knew what I wanted to be. I knew I wanted to be John Rzeznik." He sighed but not unhappily. "My life right now is actually a lot like I thought it was gonna be. If there're some things I've held on to, they're still a mystery." He kicked into a certain tone of misery that she seemed to feed off of. "I'm scared, Sara. I lost my job today."

She wrapped her arms around him and was saying, "Oh, Jamie, oh, Jamie—it's OK, it's OK," in this weird maternal way and then pulled his head to her chest.

"I'm not really worried about a job. I'm just sayin'—"

"You don't need to explain. You'll find something else—"

"I don't want to go back. I don't want to leave."

"Well, you won't have to," she said.

"How do you know that?"

"Because you have no place else to go."

They descended into the Thirty-Third Street station and Jamie could hear the screech of the 6 train's brakes from way down the tunnel, and inside him this vague fear kept growing but never really became clear—it was a kind of paranoia. They boarded the 6 and he grabbed an overhead handrail, and then the train slowly left the station and screeched through the dark and Jamie looked at the bald man, the only other passenger, sitting cross-legged in the corner seat with the fluorescent train lights illuminating the sweat on his skull and the sheen on his skin. Music was coming from the Apple earbuds he was wearing and the cord went to his hand, which was holding an iPod. Jamie changed position so that he could see the man more clearly. Tried to get a good look at him. He looked like a rough imitation of a human being and was taking deep breaths that turned into fast, short breaths, muttering something, growling, seemingly pissed about being trapped / imprisoned / ensnared in the train. Jamie moved so close to him that he could hear the bald man's muttering over the train's screeching brakes. It was quiet, but he recognized the words: *"The pony keeps running around, looking for a way out of the cage. The pony keeps running around, looking for a way out of the cage. The pony keeps running around, looking for a way out of the cage"*—and the bald man turned and made eye contact with him, looking briefly as if he'd offended him in some way, and his eyes signaled something and then something broke within the train and the emergency lights came on and the train came to a stop and everyone moaned. Jamie looked at Sara and she was looking at him like she didn't know what to do and he didn't know what to do either, so he checked his iPhone again and again and then he looked at the bald man, his face turning red, his hands shaking and eyelids trembling. Sara said something that he could barely hear.

"What? I can barely hear you," Jamie said.

"I said we should just get out and walk back on the track," she said.

"No... don't, Sara," he said, his throat tight.

He kept his eyes on the door even as the bald man's glances became stares, and for some reason the place smelled like piss all of a sudden, it smelled like shit, and the bald man swallowed and coughed and then coughed again, his breathing irregular, and in the next moment he was screaming and punching the subway door with his fists like he really needed to get off that fucking train. He was pounding his fists on the glass and howling and muttering and drooling like he'd been bitten by a dog and infected with some kind of madness, some new kind of virus or plague, like his "spiral of depersonalization had gone so deep" that—

—which caused Jamie's eyes to widen, and then he thought the bald man was either on a four- to five-day coke binge or that he was the serial killer he'd seen on CNN. He brought himself to look into the bald man's eyes—the bald man's blinking and bloodshot eyes, red because of the lights—and they just stared at each other uncertainly, both with the same red eyes, and then Jamie began to panic, as if he knew he hadn't done some indefinably deep thing with his life.

"What in the fuck is going on?" Sara said.

There was a pause.

"Just keep your head down," Jamie said. "I think he..." His voice trailed off and then he took a deep breath and was able to compose himself by staring at his feet and counting to ten or twenty. "We're gonna start movin'."

He was thinking, *Oh god, oh god, oh god, please don't let him be the serial killer.*

Over his shoulder Sara's face was creased and her eyes were watery. "I'm just like..." she said, trying to catch her breath. "I'm just like... saying we should—"

"Sara, just shut the fuck up for a sec."

The bald man looked at Jamie, and Jamie was shaking so hard he couldn't do anything and he was sure he was going to die. He just stood there and let the bald man stagger up to him, and he could feel those hands around his throat, tighter and tighter, pushing him onto the floor, killing him. He'd be like all the things in this world that shine and then, like all the things in this world, like *all* the things in this world, he'd die. But the bald man said nothing and studied Jamie's blank expression before shaking his head disgustedly and going into the corner to vomit.

And then the lights came back on.

And the train started moving down the tunnel.

And Jamie Paddock lived.

THEY EMERGED FROM THE SUBWAY station onto Eighty-Sixth Street, one of the greatest streets in the world, with restaurants and stores, beautiful women and men with their blind eyes and their deaf ears, their burned faces and missing limbs, and Jamie spread his body out on the sidewalk and laughed and felt as if he'd fallen from a great height. Looking up at the steel-gray buildings, he realized: *I'm finally back.* "We didn't die," he said, laughing. "This is... amazing." Sara sat on the ground and asked him what the fuck he was talking about, and he said, "He was that serial killer guy, Sara. That's who that was. It was that serial killer," and then she dared him to keep saying "serial killer" and called him retarded. After what seemed like hours, he stood up when the urge to fuck hit him (not all that unexpectedly, really), and over the sounds of construction and traffic he could hear someone singing Bruno Mars, and because she was still totally insane (but in a cool way), Sara rustled through his pockets as they headed west on Eighty-Sixth. He reached down, fumbling for the arrowhead, but she grabbed it first and he tried to grab her hand, but when he finally stopped fighting her she had it in her fist.

"So how'd you get this thing?" she said.

She looked, waiting. He looked for a moment as if he wouldn't go on.

"I was five or six. I was walking in the woods with my dad, it was fall..."

THE NEXT DAY JAMIE AND SARA went to the Met and ended up in a group with a bunch of kids, and when the tour guide called the kids to attention and started talking about all the different kinds of gods in ancient Egypt, Jamie found himself listening, following along where some of the kids were entering the Tomb of Perneb, and when he was inside, he dropped the arrowhead.

33

LATER, HE WALKED AIMLESSLY in the cold clear night and he got lost for a while. No one noticed. No one, he thought, paid much attention to him any longer. He stopped and looked upward and searched the sky for stars, and then he thought about going back home. But he wouldn't go back home. He wouldn't go back home to his apartment or West Virginia or his mother. Not for a while at least. Instead he'd walk the streets of the city he'd never leave.

And then one day, a text came in from his sister, and it said they'd found his father's body. So he traveled far, far away to West Virginia, as he'd traveled before.

And he went to the funeral and they raised their voices for their father.

Roy Paddock this! Roy Paddock that! Roy Paddock was!

Jamie sat there in the pews, his ass hurting, all these crazy thoughts filling his head. Thoughts about his dad, he guessed, even if his dad didn't feature in them.

And the preacher spoke with evangelical fervor.

"There is a winged creature comin' to save you," he said.

He said it would carry Jamie wherever he wanted to go.

And Jamie smiled and thought, *I'm already there.*

Acknowledgments

It's very hard to exist as part of the West Virginia psychosphere because you're always an outsider. But it's where I grew up, and I returned years later to mature as a writer. My entire "formation" is from the time I spent there, so surely *West Virginia* belongs to West Virginia.

I owe a lot to the people of Unnamed Press, to Chris and Olivia, whose talent and support are the reasons this book is in your hands. It's because of them and people like them, independent publishers who take risks, that historically marginalized voices are being amplified.

My parents, who always had a knack for making something out of nothing.

And Molly, who holds me together and loves me.

About the Author

Joe Halstead was born and raised in Mount Lookout, West Virginia. He currently lives in Lexington, Kentucky with his wife and cat. His work has appeared in *Five Quarterly, People Holding, Cheat River Review, Sundog Lit, The Stockholm Review, Sheepshead Review*, and others. *West Virginia* is his first novel.

@unnamedpress

facebook.com/theunnamedpress

unnamedpress.tumblr.com

www.unnamedpress.com